HACKBERRY
JONES,
SPLIT END

Also by Curtis Bishop

HACKBERRY JONES, SPLIT END

Curtis Bishop

J. B. LIPPINCOTT COMPANY

PHILADELPHIA AND NEW YORK

PRINTED IN THE UNITED STATES OF AMERICA

Library of Congress Catalog Card Number 68-24425

FIRST EDITION

TYPOGRAPHY BY Margaret F. Plympton

Contents

HACKBERRY JONES, SPLIT END

1

JUST ASK THE COACH

◆-◆-◆

Jim Carter was not surprised by Coach Pearson's doubtful attitude. Accept a new boy on the Riverside varsity after practice had already started, especially a youth of no previous football experience? Mr. Pearson had as much as told Jim the day before that there was no chance of such a thing.

But Mr. Pearson had agreed to at least talk to this Hackberry Jones—before practice.

"Have your boy here at a quarter to nine and I'll look him over," the coach had conceded. "But six-feet-two and a hundred and fifty pounds—that doesn't sound like football material to me. Basketball, maybe, but—well, have him here. Anything to get my quarterback off the hook with his girl friend."

Jim had telephoned Joan Morgan and she must have contacted Hack Jones, for the lanky youth was outside the Red Rover dressing room when Jim arrived. And now Jones stood dutifully answering Coach Pearson's questions.

Or rather Hack slouched, or lounged, thought Jim. This human beanpole might be an impressive figure on horseback—he worked at a riding stable near Austin, and this was how and why Joan knew him. But stand red-haired Hack Jones on his own two feet and—well, you almost didn't. He either teetered sideways or slouched forward and——

"What makes you think you can play football, Jones?"

Jim sighed and wished that Mr. Pearson would just reject this unlikely applicant and get it over with.

"Never said I could, Mr. Pearson. The fact is—I never even thought about it. But these three fillies—young ladies, I mean—are mighty good customers at the stables. And Mister Ed—he's the man I work for—says that if it'll make 'em happy for me to play a little football this year—well, just do it and charge the time to work. That's the way Mister Ed is about things. Always worrying about his customers."

Jim Carter shut his eyes and waited for the explosion. Coach Pearson was usually a mild-mannered man, but when he cut loose——!

But the mentor only said softly, "I see," and Jim guessed that Mr. Pearson meant to handle this with gentle sarcasm. Or start that way, anyhow. "Well, Jones, let's put it this way. Why are these three young ladies so sure that you can help the football team? I presume they *are* students at Riverside?"

"Yes, sir." Hack Jones was completely unabashed. Jim chuckled to himself. Unabashed—imagine his coming up with a word like that! Maybe he wouldn't have as much trouble with English this year as he had expected.

Hack shifted his feet and his body slanted in the opposite direction. "Well, sir, it was a funny thing. Some college kids started coming to the stables most every day. Fraternity boys from the University of Texas. They'd ride a while and then they'd choose up for what they called touch football. There was an odd number of 'em one day and they wanted me to play, so the sides would be even."

The youth paused. "I understand," Coach Pearson murmured. "Go on."

"Well, all they wanted me to do was to catch the football when it was pitched to me and run to the other end of the corral without anybody touching me." Hack shrugged and flashed a grin. "Shucks, I could sure do that. I got to where I was doing it just about every time. Fact is, the college kids had to start leaving me out of their game."

"The other side didn't have a chance?"

"No, sir. The other bunch sure didn't. I kind of hated it, 'cause I was getting to like their game. Anyhow, it beat walking kids too young to turn loose with horses, and that's what I was doing most of the time."

"And that is the extent of your football experience?"

"Yes, sir. Except a little back in junior high school. We

played about the same thing and called it physical train-
ing."

"You attended Eanes Junior High School, I presume,
since the stables you talk about are outside the city limits?"

"Yes, sir. I finished up at Eanes and then went sashaying
off with my brother and—well, when Mister Ed said I had
to go to high school whether I wanted to or not—there's
some sort of deal between that school district and Riverside High School."

"Yes," nodded Coach Pearson. "The Eanes district has
no high school but sends pupils here by tuition arrange-
ment. Now, you have talked quite a bit, Jones. In fact, you
have talked more than some of our best players do in an
entire season."

Again Jim Carter grinned, though he had expected Mr.
Pearson to be even more sarcastic. There was surely more
to come but Jim wanted to go on about his own business.
A dozen other Red Rover hopefuls had arrived during this
time. They had gone straight on into the dressing room.
As one of the co-captains, Jim should be setting them an
example in putting on practice uniforms with little or no
horseplay and stalling. This promised to be a big season for
him personally, if not the Riverside team, and he meant
to make the most of it.

"I'd better get suited out, Coach," Jim said.

"Yes," Mr. Pearson said calmly. "I believe I can deal
with Jones here without your help. In fact, here comes
Coach Snow—I shall just turn Mr. Jones over to him."

"Yes, sir," Jim grinned. He thought he understood the

mentor's reasoning. This Hackberry Jones should be shared with the other two coaches. Jim hated to miss Mr. Snow's first reaction but he was more concerned with his responsibilities as co-captain. Sandy Stone, the other leader, was already half clad. Sandy was a senior, too, and a two-way starter from the previous season, whereas Jim had played mostly in the defensive secondary. Right now Jim felt that the squad looked more to Sandy for leadership. Jim Carter did not resent that attitude, but he was determined to change it.

He was glad to get the load of Hackberry Jones off his shoulders and he hoped that he would hear no more about it. Joan Morgan had started back in August and had not let up through every date with Jim since. There was the *cutest* boy working at the Bar E Ranch, as the riding stables were called. He was just out of this world! Everything he said kept Joan in stitches; Lucy Spencer and Beth Jameson, too. He was enrolling in Riverside High School after missing two years of school to travel as a rodeo performer. Could Jim *imagine* a seventeen-year-old who had already won fame as a calf roper?

Hackberry was his real name—in fact, his only name. Wasn't that just wonderful? "And, Jim, you should see him catch passes and just run off and leave those fraternity boys like they were standing still. He just *has* to play on the Riverside team this year. I'd just *die* if he didn't. So would Lucy and Beth. In fact, Lucy said she would quit as head cheerleader if Hackberry didn't get a chance, at least. And you *can* do something about it, Jim Carter. We know that prospects are invited to varsity tryouts and all other newcomers assigned automatically to the B squad. But Coach Pearson doesn't *know* about Hackberry Jones. You can tell him, Jim. You're the co-captain and regular quarterback. I just *know* that Coach Pearson will consider any new boy on your request. He just *has* to."

Well, gloried Jim, he was out of that jam. He hurried and was among the first to be completely suited out. But, due to his delay outside, he wasn't dressed as soon as Sandy Stone. All ready for the morning's drill, Sandy clattered to the dressing room door and looked around him with critical eyes.

"Stir your stumps," he said gruffly and loudly. "Grandmaw is slow but she's old. Young fellows like you can still hurry up. We want to take our laps and be ready for practice at nine sharp."

"Sure," Jim chimed in, hurriedly tying his shoelaces. "You know what the rush is for. You know we just get two hours of practice. Let's make that a hundred and twenty minutes of real football."

That practice limitation was enforced strictly in all Austin high schools, if not in every corner of the Texas Interscholastic League. So were the number of workouts before the formal opening of schools. So that, Coach Pearson had explained, put it squarely up to the boys. They could have 120 minutes of actual football instruction and drill if they were finished with their laps and calisthenics before the hour. The squad willing to do that "on its own time," as the coach put it—well, Mr. Pearson had done the arith-

metic on the dressing room blackboard. Take a forty-player
squad like this, saving 10 minutes of practice—forty times
10 was 400. Sixteen practices were allowed a team before
its first game. Sixteen times 400 totaled 6,400 practice
minutes.

That many minutes of practice time were bound to make
a difference. And there was morale, besides. A squad that
was all business by its own determination was apt to be a
winning squad. "So," Mr. Pearson said, "let's have it that
way another year at Riverside. We coaches can't *make* you
do it. Your co-captains can, if you'll let them."

At exactly ten minutes to nine co-captains Jim Carter
and Sandy Stone led the squad of white-jerseyed youths
around the field. Jim wanted to favor his sore right ankle
but forced himself not to do it. The best way to get over
a stiffness was to work it out.

He saw that Mr. Snow was throwing passes to Hackberry Jones—throwing bullets, too, as the backfield coach
could do. Jim grinned as he trotted along. He sure didn't
envy the shining light of the suburban riding academy,
facing those hard shots in nothing but a tee shirt. What a
character! How had Mike Geary described the ungainly
youth who had impressed Lucy Spencer as much as he had
Joan? Oh, yes, a redheaded scarecrow. Well, this Jones
was sure all skin and bones and that mostly arms and legs.
But Jim saw that he held the throws from Mr. Snow even
though they must have jarred his stomach muscles.

Mr. Snow could chunk. He was just three years out of
Baylor University, where he had been starting quarterback

for a time. Jim had heard that only a badly injured knee had stopped Andrew Snow from earning All-American honors and stardom in the professional game. Anybody who had ever struggled with Mr. Snow's passes found that easy to believe. There—he shot the ball at Hackberry again. The backfield coach must have showed Jones what a button-hook was, for the lanky youth whirled and took Mr. Snow's pass knee-high, as the buttonhook should be fired. Jones held the throw, marveled Jim. The redhead either slipped to his knees or was knocked there by the force of the coach's peg. But he held the pass.

Now the Rover hopefuls were starting their second lap. Jim looked back over his shoulders. There weren't any stragglers. Even Steve Peterson and Joe Kotura were keeping up.

"Now you're moving, Joe, boy," Jim called out encouragingly. He meant to do a lot of that, every time it was deserved, in fact. Sandy was stingy with his expressions of approval. Jim believed that a good captain was a "holler guy" along with his driving. He would never forget the example of his first year, and quarterback Ray Brasher. As an awkward sophomore Jim had seldom done anything right. But Brasher had observed and praised every successful effort, even though Jim would not play a down that season and both knew it.

Jim looked back again, all along the moving line. He sighed. He couldn't dispute the appraisal of the *American*'s sports writers. Riverside was not loaded this year. The squad was too light and inexperienced to be reckoned a championship contender. It was short on speed, too, without a single breakaway runner. The Crimson would have to grind out its yardage.

The quarterback post was a major weakness, according to the *American*. Jim had winced at that, for he was the quarterback. Oh, sophomore Bill Baxter was a flashy prospect, throwing well and running like a whirling dervish. But Bill weighed exactly one hundred and thirty-six pounds. He could outthrow Jim, sure. So could Rich Conover, now stationed at left halfback. But for ball-handling, play judgment, and especially for blocking, Jim Carter was the only Rover who could flip off the ball and then turn an opposing tackle or end. And he was far better at faking than the inexperienced Baxter.

He wouldn't rate a college athletic scholarship as a quarterback prospect; Jim knew that. But he knew that college talent scouts favored high-school quarterbacks for other college assignments, even line posts. The reasoning, according to Mr. Snow, was that the average high-school quarterback was a versatile all-around performer who had proved his dedication and dependability. Give a college coach thirty or forty such players and he would come up with a strong team. "Show that you're rugged and a hard worker," Mr. Snow had said, "and some major university will take a chance on your development at another position."

Well, Jim was rugged and he would work. He weighed a hundred and ninety pounds even if he stood only five-eleven. He had been an outside linebacker on defense the year before. And this season he would prove that he was also a leader.

The second lap finished, he and Sandy started the squad on calisthenics. Now, he noticed, Mr. Pearson was also involved in the passing activities of Hackberry Jones and the backfield coach. Good Lord, were they seriously considering this freak as a varsity prospect!

Seconds later he knew so. He signaled the end of exercises and went to tell Mr. Pearson that his Red Rovers were ready for official practice.

The head coach stood talking to Mr. Snow. Hackberry sat cross-legged on the edge of the cinder track, breathing a bit heavily.

"I never saw a better natural receiver," Mr. Snow was saying. "As for moves, he can pull a different trick every time. I told him to act as if he must get away from an imaginary guard and he must have showed me fifty different ways to do it. Let me have a boy to cover him and I'll show you."

"No need to," Mr. Pearson said, rubbing his chin. "I watched him."

"He reminds me a lot of Larry Elkins when I was at Baylor," Mr. Snow continued. And no doubt of it, realized Jim; the backfield coach was enthusiastic. "As for catching the ball, I couldn't *make* him drop one. And I threw some hard ones."

"I saw that, too," nodded Coach Pearson. "I don't know what we can do with him this year, but—well, he does have natural ability, plus another year, and we do have an extra uniform." He hesitated, then called out, "Julius?"

Julius Koen, the bespectacled student manager, hurried up. "Yes, sir?"

The coach pointed to the relaxed Jones. "That's Hackberry Jones. Take him over. Give him a jersey in the eighties if we have one left. And get him an appointment with Dr. Bradford. We can't let him practice until he has had a physical examination."

Jim Carter shut his eyes tight and shook his head. Joan would never let him hear the last of this. Hadn't she told him so! All he had to do was to ask the coach and Hackberry Jones would be on the Riverside varsity just like that!

2

TAUGHT BY GOATS!

◆ ◆ ◆

"I'm mighty obliged to you," Hackberry Jones told Jim Carter. "The coaching man—he wasn't too friendly to start with. I thought he was going to tell me no right off and hear no more about it. But you being captain—that's like being a foreman, isn't it?"

Jim nodded. He supposed it was, except that he doubted if cowboy crews chose their own leaders. But he was careful not to point out this difference. He had learned already that he should not encourage Hackberry to talk. Enough of that poured out without any sort of prompting.

Jones had attached himself to Jim, no doubt of it. He came to Jim for help with his shoulder pads. Jim sighed. Had Joan promised that he would do any more for Hackberry than introduce him to Coach Pearson? There was no telling what she had committed Jim to do for this new-comer to Riverside. What was it about this character which fascinated her so? Joan was just *crazy* about him and made no bones about it. Then why didn't she go with him, Jim had demanded finally. Who would not resent his date raving about another boy all evening? Oh, she did not feel *that* way about him, Joan had retorted impatiently. Wait until he knew Hack better; then Jim would understand.

Jim took a deep breath. He doubted that. He was not as wild about horseback riding as Joan and her two best friends, Lucy and Beth. He had ridden with her twice, then had sworn off. It was sort of fun, all right, but not worth any two dollars an hour, not with as little money as he had to spend. And owning and boarding her own horse, an impressive palomino—good grief, what his daughter's hobby must cost Joan's father! Granting that at the stables Hack was a real master, none of that quality showed up elsewhere.

The student manager had hustled all the necessary gear for this newest Red Rover, but none of it fitted Hackberry. Julius Koen could not do the impossible. Instead of fitting snugly over Hackberry's shoulders, the pads simply bulged there. The practice pants provided for the recruit came barely to his knees. As for the cleated shoes, the only pair big enough were those worn two seasons before by a 270-pound lineman. The practice helmet flopped loosely—Jones's head was shaped just like a bullet, according to Julius.

The net result, decided Jim, was that the uniform made

Hackberry look even less like a football player, and more like a scarecrow.

But there he was—number eighty-nine—hovering as close to Jim Carter as a young chick to its mother hen. Hack was right on his heels as Jim started the warmup laps.

This was the afternoon drill and Jim was hurrying his charges to meet a five p.m. deadline. Hack had returned with clearance from Dr. Bradford. How? Jones did not appear sturdy enough to resist a strong puff of wind. How would he fare in the tougher drills, such as one-on-one tackling and two-on-one blocking? Jim could not help grinning in anticipation. But that would have to wait until the next morning's practice. These afternoon or second sessions were given up entirely to defensive drills, at least so far. Next week they would be nearly all scrimmages.

The laps taken and exercises done, all ends and backs lined up for passing drill while interior linemen were schooled on their blocking assignments. Jim, Bill Baxter, and Rich Conover took turns throwing under Coach Snow's supervision. Conover would pass from his halfback post. The Rovers had three plays for this, and Jim considered one especially a honey. Rich, who was left-handed, would throw out of what started as a double reverse.

It fell to Jim to pass first to Hackberry—it would, he groaned inwardly.

"Buttonhook," called out Mr. Snow. The Rovers had four types of passing patterns—flair, buttonhook, sideline, and center break. The only "bomb" in their repertory would be thrown by Conover out of that reverse with only left end Dick Eudaly down.

It wasn't an ambitious passing schedule, but the Red Rovers would not count much on aerials. Mr. Pearson was known for his skepticism about the value of forward passing. Oh, he would open up if he had the material; Riverside's championship team of two years before had thrown the ball from every spot on the field. But that squad had boasted Ray Brasher, a sure marksman and also a great scrambler.

Jim took the snap from center Bob Crawford, faded, turned and threw on a count of four. His pass was a perfect spiral, one of his better efforts. But still he threw too much behind Jones for the receiver to have a chance.

Jim looked quickly at Coach Snow. Hackberry must not have run the pattern right. The end was supposed to take five steps, then cut sharply inside and take the ball facing the scrimmage line.

"He was letter perfect, Carter," the backfield coach pointed out. "You just didn't give him enough lead, or throw deep enough. Your pass would have been fine for Eudaly or Chalmers, right on the money. But this is Jones, remember—Hackberry Jones. I'll throw him a buttonhook to show what I mean. You watch this, too, Baxter. Jones, line up again. Start on a two count."

Mr. Snow knelt behind Crawford. "Down, ready," chanted the coach. "One—two——"

The intent Jim saw Jones fairly leap out of his slouching stance. Coach Snow took the usual four steps, eyes apparently fixed out to his right. Then he whirled and fired. His bullet thudded squarely into Hackberry's chest, sending the receiver toppling backward.

The difference was perfectly clear. In his five steps Jones had covered at least eight yards. His sharp cut and leap to his right was for at least six feet. Jim shook his head. No wonder he had thrown behind and short.

"Jones doesn't run with regular steps," the coach explained, "but with leaps." Mr. Snow hesitated, then added with a smile, "You see, he imitates goats."

Jim frowned. "Did you say—goats?"

"That's right," the coach said drily. "At least, that's what he told me this morning. Ask him about it when you have ten or fifteen minutes to spare, but not now. Anyhow, he does cover more ground in fewer steps than any receiver *I* was ever used to. You try that buttonhook with him, Baxter."

Jim stepped aside and watched with tight lips. It was a struggle not to show his resentment. Of course the slight sophomore would throw the pattern better. In the first place, Jim had to admit, Baxter was the better passer. Then, too, Bill could profit from the two previous examples. He would know to give the receiver an unusual lead.

Bill crouched behind Bob Crawford, took the ball, faded and threw. Hackberry had executed his sharp turn. He had to dive back for the ball. He caught it knee-high and fell flat.

"Golly," said Bill Baxter as if he could not believe it. "I still underthrew."

"But it could still be caught," Jim muttered to Rich Conover.

"He is almost unbelievable," Mr. Snow told Bill. "But I can believe it; we had a receiver like that at Baylor." He squeezed Bill's shoulder. "We'll have him with us on the second team, Bill. We'll cook up a fresh pattern or two for him. Maybe we can bother these high and mighty first stringers next week."

"We sure can," Bill said with a grin.

The flair, the sideline, then the halfback pass. It was Mutt Allison's turn to receive but Coach Snow interrupted. He gestured to Hackberry.

"You take this turn, Jones. I want to see if Conover can throw to you. At the count you angle out, then cut back some and head downfield as fast as you can. Look back at the count of seven. Conover will throw then if you're loose. He'll throw high so all you have to do is to run under the ball."

"You mean—fake this way, then take off like a sage hen?"

"Exactly," nodded the backfield coach. "This is our bomb, Jones, the only one we have so far."

Jim crouched behind Crawford for the snap. Conover went into motion to his right, but he cut back sharply on "set." Jim faked a handoff to Mike Geary, then pitched deep to Conover. The halfback ran four or five steps with the ball, then set himself to throw. By then Hackberry Jones was over forty yards downfield. Rich threw mightily, but Jones had to stop and wait for the ball.

"You got it to him," Jim said to Rich, "and that's more than I did."

"But just because he waited for it. You know, Jim, that scarecrow billy goat is making us look more like second-stringers every day."

Mr. Pearson now had joined Coach Snow, leaving the drill of linemen to the veteran line coach, Chris Zanoba.

"You see, Coach," Mr. Snow said, "it's just as I thought. In seven seconds Jones will be out of the range of any high-school passer. But we can't do the ball handling any faster. I'll just have to work out a special pattern for Jones. He can cut all the way to the sidelines, then back."

"He gets down the field," agreed Mr. Pearson. His eyes twinkled. "I wonder how fast he can do the hundred, if he can be taught to run straight. I've given Coach Edwards fair warning. Jones will help the track team even if he won't be much good to us."

"We can use Jones," Mr. Snow said slowly, "and this year. He can be taught. He listens well—when he isn't talking to himself."

Jones was now back in his easy lope. "That boy will have to throw harder than that, Mr. Snow," the red-haired youth said. "That was the trouble I had with those college boys. None of 'em could throw far enough."

"Enough of that, Jones," Mr. Snow said firmly. "Con-over threw at least forty-five yards and that's all we can expect. I'll just have to give you a special pattern, that's all. Come with me now. All you others on the second-string offense, too. We'll go down in the end zone and see if we can't cook up something for Coach Pearson's varsity."

"Well, at least they haven't forgotten about keeping us all on our toes with breathing down each other's neck," Jim remarked to Rich as they walked toward Mr. Pearson. "That helped a lot last year. But now these special patterns for Mr. Jones—did you hear that character bragging—'that's the trouble I had with those college boys.' Sometimes I just feel like hitting him."

"Forget that, Jim," Rich cautioned him. "He didn't really *sound* braggy. At least I don't think he meant to. And he did outrun anything I could throw to him. Anyway, it looks as if we've got to live with him, like it or not."

Mr. Pearson and Chris Zanoba, the line coach, began sending the offensive starters through their paces. None had any guarantee on his position, of course. No later than Monday afternoon each of the eleven would be battling to keep his place. Those scrimmages might bring out any number of changes. Jim believed two regulars would give way to junior challengers, end Mutt Allison and right guard Jack Bowen. But Jim did not believe the competition would be too close for the other assignments.

We have the makings of a good club, he decided, regardless of how the so-called experts rated Riverside in city and district competition. Theirs would be a consistent attack out of the Regular T, if not a flashy one. Coach Pearson had considered shifting to the I formation and Jim wished the coach had done so. For the Crimson strength was between the tackles. Both Geary and right half Chester

Gordon were fairly strong runners. Give either a slight
opening and he would add a yard on his own. And Conover
was getting better every day. If he could be taught how and
when to cut, he would register many a gain on the power
sweep.

The Rovers ran through every play twice, then were allowed a breather while Mr. Zanoba arranged a defense
from the "ragnots," the sophomores and juniors he wanted
to develop for next year. Jim watched the assignment of
positions closely. Most of these eleven boys had played for
the B squad the year before; only tackle Doug Prewitt and
guard Red Billings had varsity experience. That and the
average fifteen-pound weight advantage should make this
an easy scrimmage test. Riverside might have the material
for two platoons, but not three.

But still it was scrimmage; these ragnots would not back
off and let the varsity romp. Each wore a sleeveless red
shirt over his practice jersey.

Jim was free to call his own plays. He tried the belly
series first; he considered that their bread-and-butter offense. Most of their success would depend on his ball handling. He did that well, and he knew it. On the crisscross
and follow patterns he had the ragnots tackling the wrong
back consistently.

The Crimsons gained almost every play. More important, they were getting off with the snap. Jim mixed in a
few forward passes, short ones. Twice he threw the jump
to Dick Eudaly. He shot a perfect look-in to Allison. But
his effort to hit the same receiver on a sideline pattern

brought disaster. His throw was a bit short and was intercepted by sophomore Steve Goodman, whose older brother was first understudy to Sandy Stone. Steve would have gone all the way if he hadn't been stopped by Coach Pearson's impatient whistle.

That interception discouraged Jim; it was all he could do to keep from showing it. The blame was all his, for his teammates had given him ample protection. It just proved again that he was not much of a passer. He must restrict what throwing he did to look-ins and jumps, he decided, and depend on the halfback passes.

Mr. Pearson called a halt after two more plays. His blue eyes fairly glinted as he coldly recited their faults.

"I can't say much for your offense, Jim," he concluded. "If it doesn't improve next week, you so-called regulars are going to have a hard time. Mr. Zanoba's first defensive platoon will stop you dead. And I expect Mr. Snow to have a fair little second offense by Monday. You may be showed up on both offense and defense next week."

He ordered each player to review his assignments before the next afternoon's drill.

"That's all for today," he said.

Most of the chagrined regulars headed for the dressing room, but not Jim. As a co-captain he would be the last Red Rover into the dressing room, and Mr. Snow was still working his second unit. Jim was surprised to see that Hackberry Jones was running as a split end, a wide split end. How could the gangling boy have already earned a place on the second team?

Then, as Jim watched, Bill Baxter faded and threw a perfect sideline which Jones gathered in just before stepping out of bounds. Jim sighed. He could not make that play work, and the second-stringers made it look easy. Their offense, he had to concede after a minute, seemed to have a smoother execution than that of the varsity. But they haven't faced actual competition, Jim muttered to himself. Just wait until next week's headknocking against the varsity. Then young Mr. Baxter would find out that quarterbacking against the south breeze was far different than against strong opposition.

Mr. Snow dismissed his charges, too, but with words of praise instead of cold criticism.

Jim scowled as he trotted toward the dressing room. He must warn his teammates, he brooded. They had better be sharp next week or there would be some new faces in the starting lineup. Maybe even he didn't have his position cinched. No, he decided, Bill Baxter was just too slight and too young. He would not play much this season, no matter how smoothly he executed assignments or threw passes. High-school sophomores just didn't take over the quarterback's post from a senior.

Jim had no more than stripped off his sweat-soaked togs than Hackberry Jones was in his hair again. Would Jim help him with his jersey? It didn't seem to want to come off. Jim yanked and the wet garment came over the shoulder pads and Hackberry could manage the rest.

"This football is sort of fun," Hackberry said, grinning.

"I just had a real good time today. That Mr. Snow—he sure knows how to organize things."

"It won't be so easy in the morning," Jim promised. "You haven't done any one-on-one blocking or tackling yet."

Jim explained what those terms meant as best he could when the redhead looked puzzled. Hackberry's features registered surprise.

"Couldn't somebody get hurt doing that?"

Jim grunted. Hurt was right, jarred to the eyeteeth even when not actually injured.

"I don't think we ought to try to hurt each other," Jones protested.

"Football is rough," Jim told him. "That's the only way to play it. And hitting hard is the only way to keep from being hurt."

"I dunno," muttered Hack. "I just hope nobody hurts me out there. I might get mad and——"

"And what?" Jim demanded with a grin. What would Jones do to teammates who outweighed him thirty to sixty pounds?

He didn't know, Hackberry confessed.

Jim suddenly remembered Coach Snow's suggestion. Now was a good time to ask Hackberry how he could have learned his pass-receiving maneuvers from watching goats.

"By watching 'em," Jones said, "and then acting like one."

He was not hesitant with his full explanation. He had this older brother. They had lived on a hill-country ranch until four years ago. His brother had set out to make a rodeo star of Hackberry, especially as a roper. Not having any calves to practice with, the two of them had used goats.

"It's plumb good practice," Hackberry explained. "The best there is. When you can rope a goat, you can catch anything. But they aren't real sturdy animals, not in the legs, anyhow. It isn't hard at all to bust a goat's leg, especially when you're hurrying to tie three legs. My brother ruined three or four goats and Paw hit the ceiling. No more goat roping, he said, not his goats, anyhow. How could we practice, my brother wanted to know. Paw just grunted. 'You fool kids rope each other,' he said. 'One of you gets hurt and we ain't out much.'"

Hackberry paused for breath. "And that's just what we did, except it was me mostly—getting roped, I mean. My brother chased me all over the corral every chance we had. I got to making a game out of it. I got to cutting this way and that and bolting straight ahead—got to be about as fast and tricky as a goat. Sometimes he'd have to throw two or three loops to catch me. And my brother was a good roper, plenty good."

Jim hesitated. Did Jones mean what he had said?

"Your brother—*was?*"

"Yep," nodded Hackberry. "Killed at Cheyenne. Bull-dogging. Missed clean and—well, he never was much of a dogger. Nothing to practice on. I sure couldn't make like a Brahman steer."

3

JIM SENSES TROUBLE

❖ ❖ ❖

Jim Carter tried not to grin. He should pity Hackberry Jones instead of enjoying the redhead's misery.

For this was dummy drill with assistant coach Chris Zanoba in charge. Riverside squads spent more time blocking and tackling dummies than most high-school groups— Jim knew that from conversations with youths who played for Travis or McCallum or North Side. Heavyset, graying Coach Zanoba believed in "hard-nosed" football and he usually had his Red Rover defenses playing it by mid-September.

The Red Rover sentiment was unanimous. The minutes spent under Coach Zanoba were the hardest part of any workout. Sure they suffered; the line coach admitted so cheerfully. They were supposed to. That was the grim dull toil of football. It separated the men from the boys, claimed Chris Zanoba. Teaching knuckleheads how to block and tackle was his business, and he worked hard at it.

But he couldn't do anything with Hackberry Jones. The line coach said so after a few exasperating moments.

Jim was sure that he would never forget Hackberry's first "charge." The lanky youth sort of sidled up to the dummy and gave it a sidewise swipe.

The Red Rovers knew what was coming. And they were not disappointed.

"Jones, that is the poorest excuse for a block I ever saw. You couldn't block out a *girl* that way. I'll show you one more time."

The line coach might be approaching fifty but he could still hurl his full weight against a dummy. When he hit, the padded thing fairly shook, as if it had human feelings after all.

"See?" demanded Mr. Zanoba, scrambling to his feet.

Jim saw Hackberry's lips tighten. The human beanpole nodded. But he had only seen, he had not learned. He sprawled off the dummy in a glancing block.

"Look, Jones," snapped the line coach. "Mr. Snow wants you to play end. He thinks you are cute catching a pass, and maybe you are. But how can you play end if you can't turn a tackle or carry out a linebacker?" The mentor grabbed the dummy himself. "This time, tear into it," he ordered. He braced his feet. "There's a lap for you unless you can move me."

That was hardly a fair test, thought Jim. Mr. Zanoba was

not easy to budge. Jim had done it a few times, as had Sandy Stone, Mike Geary and Joe Kotura. But to most Rovers, hitting the dummy braced by Coach Zanoba was like colliding with a stone wall.

Hackberry did no better. He just didn't want to hit and there was no doubt about it.

"All right, take that lap," Mr. Zanoba said disgustedly. "And it's all right with me if you keep on running."

Tackling was the same.

"You just don't *hug*, Jones. You *hit* it and hold on. You're grabbing it as if it's a girl on your first date and you're scared of getting slapped. Try again."

No better result.

"Jones, I give up," Mr. Zanoba sighed. "I'm trying to teach you for your own good, Son. You'll get killed in one-on-one or scrimmage unless you listen to me. You can't *sneak* up on a ball carrier. He can see you. He's going to hit you with his knees up and his helmet down and there'll be pieces of you scattered all over the field."

Jim could not decide about Hackberry's reaction. The skinny youth listened and watched and appeared to be doing his best. And not once did he answer back, not until the line coach demanded in an impatient voice:

"Jones, don't you ever get *mad*?"

"I sure try not to, Mr. Zanoba," Hackberry said evenly. "I get sorta sick inside when I do."

The line coach's black eyes glittered. "You get sick inside!" he mocked. "Well, you're gonna be sick all over after you've been busted a time or two in scrimmage.

Coach Snow is dead wrong about you, Jones. You'll never
make an end. You're not going to live long enough!"

No, he shouldn't grin, Jim admitted. He should recall
his own first session under Chris Zanoba and sympathize
with Jones. But all the same, he wished Joan were here to
see and hear for herself. Then maybe she wouldn't be so
sure that her red-haired idol was going to be such a "wonderful" player.

She had telephoned Jim the night before. He had not
really been glad to hear her voice. He knew what she would
ask and then what she would say. Sure enough, her very
first question was whether Hackberry had been accepted
on the varsity. Jim had answered truthfully. What else
could he do?

"Oh, I'm so glad," she had exclaimed. "For the team's
sake. He'll make a wonderful player, you wait and see. All
you'll have to do, Jim, is to throw him the ball. Lucy and
Beth will be as excited as I am. I can't wait to tell them."

The one-on-one tackling drill showed even more clearly
that Hackberry did not like body contact. He would let
others hit him, but Mr. Zanoba got nowhere in his effort
to make Jones charge head-on. One-on-one was the worst
part of any practice. Ball carrier and tackler squared off
against each other only four feet apart. They charged each
other between markers only three feet apart. The purpose
was twofold. First, defensive players were trained to tackle
so hard that they prevented ball carriers from lunging forward their full length after contact. And for the ball car-

riers, there was valuable practice in shifting from the full
force of a tackle and holding on to the ball.

The two opposite lines formed without regard for position or size. Hackberry was overmatched, true. He drew
Mike Geary for the first test. But Geary wouldn't have
driven clear past Jones, breaking free, if the recruit had not
tried to tackle with only his arms. Dick Eudaly and Bob
Crawford handled Jones the same way. And, on his turns
as ball carrier, Hackberry went limp on contact instead of
straining for another few inches.

Jim could not help gloating over Hackberry's poor showing. Why shouldn't there be something hard for him in
football? Why should he just saunter out after practice had
already started and step right into stardom? Jim had won
his starting position the hard way. Wasn't it fitting that
Jones should find something hard and discouraging? If his
cheerful self-confidence wasn't jarred, then it should be.
For Hackberry Jones just might not prove a "wonderful"
player overnight. How could he do that if Mr. Zanoba
wrung his neck before the season opened? And the assistant coach might do just that any minute now.

The last half hour of the workout was easier. For Jones,
it was full idleness. Mr. Zanoba refused even to assign the
skinny youth to a defensive berth.

"The way you tackle, Jones," the line coach growled,
"I'd be ashamed to see you on the field in a Riverside jersey."

Hackberry did not appear too discouraged, noticed Jim.

"I don't get it," he grunted to Rich Conover. "He doesn't even seem to care. I think he's just plain scared yellow."

"Aw, Jim, you don't know that," Rich pointed out. "But I'll tell you one thing for sure—that scarecrow is sure different, just plain weird."

Most of the Rovers already knew the defensive patterns from the year before. They would add only one new maneuver, said Mr. Zanoba, the safety blitz. The Rovers would borrow that page from the book of the professional St. Louis Cardinals. One of the two safety men would blitz on most first down plays by the opposition.

It had surprised Jim to learn from Coach Snow that such defensive patterns had been used only since the 1940's. They had been a part of football ever since he could remember. His coaches had taught him shifting defensive patterns even in the Pop Warner league. Always he had played in the secondary, either as a linebacker or a defensive halfback.

The 6-3-2 was Riverside's basic pattern. But Mr. Zanoba taught his linemen to jitterburg and his linebackers to fall in and out of the first line of defense. The middle linebacker called signals, when a substitute didn't bring in instructions from the bench.

Riverside was starting out with two platoons, as usual. So it had been in Jim's sophomore and junior years, too, but some players had ended up doing double duty. Jim meant to play both ways himself, and he was sure that Sandy Stone would do the same. Riverside just didn't have enough material to field two strong starting lineups, not unless this year was an exception.

Two platoons and the third group, the ragnots, would work as separate combinations until the coaches were fully satisfied about their individual abilities. And, Jim knew, there might be some experience for all three units this year. Even the ragnots could hope for some game action, for Mr. Zanoba would have them able to stop easy touchdowns by the end of the next week, if they couldn't do it now. And the second unit would be hard competition for the offensive starters this very week. A defense always developed more quickly then the offense.

Mr. Zanoba was satisfied with still a quarter hour left.

"You could stop the Green Bay Packers—on paper," he said gruffly. "We'll see Monday what you can really do."

Half the squad was dismissed, but not Jim Carter nor Mr. Snow's second-string offensive unit. Mr. Jones was ordered up from the soft grass and into action again. Chris Zanoba might have despaired of ever putting the redhead to good use, but not Coach Snow.

For Jim it was more punting and place-kicking practice. The latter was a new duty for him, something he had practiced all summer. It sure wouldn't hurt his college chances if he could boot extra points and field goals. Some boys landed full scholarships as kicking specialists.

Rich Conover was being groomed to hold. If he could master this duty, which was just as important as the kicking, then Riverside could add a fake place-kick to its repertory. Rich could take the pass from center but rise up to pass instead of placing the ball on the kicking tee.

So far Rich was doing well enough, though he had to hold the ball one way for Jim and another for Bob Crawford. Bob wanted the pigskin slanted backwards. It had to be straight up for Jim, as he had learned to kick like a soccer player. A neighbor and former Rover star, Claude Berry, had quit football in favor of soccer at the United States Military Academy. Claude had persuaded Jim that the sidewise kick was the best. He had to strip off his right shoe to kick so, but that was no problem.

He should be given the nod over Bob if their abilities proved about the same, for Crawford was needed to pass the ball back from center.

Between kicks Jim watched Coach Snow's offensive drill at the opposite end of the field. He saw that Hackberry was still lining up as a split end. And wingback Ed Holloway was going into motion wide on almost every play. That converted the Regular T into a pro-style formation. It was a smart move, in Jim's opinion, even if the Crimson did not use the spread in any games. It would help the Rovers to scrimmage against a split-end, slot-back attack, which most high schools used. Both North Side and McCallum, their arch rivals, used no other formation except for punts. If the Rover defense unit worked against the spread in every workout——

Except it would not be a separate unit. Jim Carter would be a linebacker in it as well as quarterback on offense. And he would be punter and place-kicker. Would college scouts please note? This Carter kid did everything for his team except carry the water bucket and administer first aid!

Then it was Monday afternoon and time for the first full-scale scrimmage. Jim knew from past experience that he and his mates on offense would have a hard time of it. Chris Zanoba's defense would work more smoothly than the Crimson attack.

But it was worse than Jim had expected. For one thing, he quickly realized, he had underestimated several youths in the defensive lineup. Jeb Savage, Doug Prewitt, Jack Mitchell, Red Billings—golly, they had improved since their sophomore seasons. They were bigger, tougher, smarter. The boys wearing sleeveless red shirts were in on Jim with the snap of the ball. Mr. Zanoba directed the defense from the center of the field, and it wasn't the same any two consecutive plays. The offensive linemen found it difficult to execute their blocks against the jitterbugging. They were accustomed to blocking a stationary dummy, not an elusive human rival.

And, of course, these defensive players knew the plays as well as Jim and his teammates did.

Twice the Redshirts held. There was no punting on fourth down; this was only practice. But the white-jerseyed group could not gain ten yards on four running plays, much less three.

Gordon on the halfback follow—that was the only sure gainer. Then Jim cleared Conover on the power sweep, taking out the defensive end single-handed. And the jump pass clicked in one out of three attempts. Once Eudaly dropped a perfect throw; once Jim passed poorly. But there were only three first downs to show for as many possessions of the ball—a chagrined Jim Carter led his team to the sidelines for a sip of water and a look at what the second offense did.

Jim's lips grew drier and drier as he watched.

The spread did not pass Chris Zanoba's defense. A halfback moved out to cover Hackberry Jones and a linebacker shifted over as Ed Holloway went into motion. And defensive halfback Steve Goodman was right there when Hackberry cut and turned on the look-in. Steve tackled Jones almost as soon as the beanpole took the throw from Baxter.

Jim's lips tightened as he saw Jones collapse immediately on contact. The lanky youth seemed to wince even before he was hit.

But still the play gained six yards and a sideline shot to the same split end netted five and a first down. Both passes by sophomore Baxter were true shots, and both were caught cleanly.

Jim shook his head. Why couldn't he throw like that! This Baxter kid, as skinny as Hackberry Jones, but nowhere near as tall, would be another Ray Brasher before he finished Riverside. If he could stand the punishment, that was. There was plenty of that coming to him. It started the very next play. Two linebackers moved into the line before the snap, making an eight-man forward wall. Bud Jameson and Jack Mitchell rushed, too. They were in on Baxter as he fell back. Jameson was halted for an instant by Pete Miller, the second-string fullback. But Mitchell bore on in and he weighed a hundred and ninety pounds. He waved his arms high so that Bill could not make his throw. He caught the quarterback by the shoulder pads as Baxter tried to dart away. Bill was slammed to the turf with tackle Doug Prewitt hitting a split second behind Mitchell.

Almost four hundred pounds of solid driving force! But Bill Baxter scrambled to his feet without a second's hesitation. Jim shook his head. This pint-sized boy would not get up every time. Bill would just have to grow some before he played on even terms with the big boys.

The same spread was used again, but Pete was boring into the line. Then Pat Wayne went off tackle on the crisscross—or tried to. Prewitt and Billy Cox caught the ball carrier between them and hurled him back.

Then there was another look-in to Hackberry. Bill had to throw too quickly and Jones was forced to dive backward to take the pass. But he caught it just before sprawling at full length. The gain was far short of a first down and Jack Mitchell whooped approval. He called to Coach Snow in a voice loud enough for Jim and his teammates to hear.

"You got another offensive unit, Coach? These boys are just as easy as that other bunch."

Jim grinned ruefully, remembering last year. Then, as a defensive player, he had voiced similar taunts in early scrimmages. But it wouldn't last, he was tempted to shout back. The offensive units would improve every day from now on. It took this sort of competition in practice to teach them what they had to learn.

In fact, Jim was just plain pleased with the showing of Mitchell, Prewitt, and the others. Usually Riverside had to give away reserve strength to its rivals. Take the previous year. Injuries to three starting players had cost the Red Rovers any chance there had been of beating North Side. Their replacements had been inadequate. Maybe it would be different this year.

Coach Pearson stood on the sidelines watching with his arms folded. Apparently he meant to trust his two assistants to do most of the actual instructing. Both were busy on the field, Mr. Snow in every huddle, Chris Zanoba right in the middle of his defense, urging them to hit even harder.

Jim went to the water can for a short sip. Mr. Pearson gestured to him. "Carter?"

"Yes, sir?" Was the coach going to try him with the second unit or on defense? Jim was eager to do either.

"You did us a good turn when you brought Jones around."

"You really think so, Coach? I'm glad. But do you think he can help us this year?" He wanted to add, "even if he is afraid of contact," but did not quite dare.

"He has Coach Snow babbling about changing our offense," Mr. Pearson said with a smile. "And I am just about ready to give in to him. Three passes, three completions—you can't beat that."

Jim had to agree. A 50 percent completion record was
enough to make a passing game click.

"But his blocking," Jim had to point out. "He won't hit
and——"

Coach Pearson pointed to the field. Jones was split wide
again with halfback Steve Goodman now playing him almost shoulder to shoulder. Pat Wayne wriggled for three
yards on the halfback follow.

"Why expect him to block? Isn't he taking a defensive
man out of every play?"

Jim did not answer at once, but he could not argue.

"And so far he has gained more yards than Wayne and
Miller put together," the coach added. "Watch this spread
formation closely, Jim. The varsity may be trying it tomorrow or the next day."

"With Jones as split end?" Jim hoped his voice did not
sound as weak as he felt. That just couldn't happen. Hackberry just couldn't saunter out so nonchalantly and slouch
his way into the starting lineup.

"Of course," Mr. Pearson said calmly. "The formation
isn't sound without a talented pass receiver, one who can
get away from any defensive halfback. There should be
two such strong receiving threats, in fact. We'll work more
with Rich this week. Mr. Snow believes in his possibilities
as a slot back, if he can be taught more deceptive moves.
Maybe he can, with Jones to show him what to do."

Jim had to put his hand over his mouth to hide his grin.
Imagine Rich taking lessons from Hackberry! What if he
told Lucy Spencer that her steady boyfriend was taking

football pointers from a beanpole cowboy who had learned the game from goats! He would have Rich to fight. Rich and Mike Geary had not said much about it, but Jim knew they were as tired of hearing about Hackberry Jones as he was.

"And Holloway is taking to this spread like a duck to water," the coach added, his eyes gleaming with pleasure.

By coincidence Ed proved that as coach and player stood and watched, before the startled Jim could voice reaction about this implied threat to Conover's starting position. Bill Baxter faded with the ball and he had time to pick his target. He faked a throw to Jones out in the flat, then wheeled and fired to Holloway, who had broken straight over center. The pass was no bullet. Ed was wide open, so Baxter just sailed the ball. Ed took it head high without slackening his stride. The second-string wingback broke away from Don Wilson and was out in the clear except for Steve Goodman, who was angling over hard and fast. But the runner moved a full thirty more yards before being driven out of bounds.

"You see, Jim?" Mr. Pearson asked his co-captain. "We may develop an offense yet. And did you notice how Baxter faked one way and then threw another? That helped a lot. And when he spotted his receiver wide open, he eased up on his throw. It helps a passer to use his head as well as his throwing arm, Jim. Remember Bobby Layne, the pro star? He never was an exceptional passer. But he could pick his receivers and he threw the pass he had to."

"Yes, sir," Jim answered quietly.

He took a deep breath. This was a fine turn of events. While Rich Conover was "learning" from Hackberry Jones, Jim Carter would be taking lessons from a sophomore!

4

AN
UNHAPPY TURN
OF EVENTS

❖ ❖ ❖

The next morning Mr. Pearson called his charges into a skull session and quickly covered the blackboard with X's. Jim grunted. Here it was—the split-end, slot-back formation. The coach certainly wasn't wasting any time. Jim glanced sideways at Bill Baxter. The sophomore was grinning.

"We're adding split-end plays starting this afternoon," Mr. Pearson said. "We'll add a play or a variation a day until Thursday. We start with the quarterback option. Mr. Snow has already taught it to his unit, and taught it well. They crammed it down the throats of our so-called first team yesterday."

A chorus interrupted him, cheers from the second stringers. Neither Mr. Pearson nor the other coaches objected. Jim scowled. The mentors surely did like to build up this early season rivalry between the two units. The second team was praised at every turn while varsity players heard little but what they did wrong.

"The lineblocking assignments are the same as on the option we already know—or should know. What is your assignment, Kotura?"

The heavyset right guard blinked, then looked to Mr. Zanoba.

"The quarterback option, Kotura," the line coach snapped. "Do you block, go downfield for a pass or run over to the sidelines and hug a cheerleader?"

"I hold the middle guard for a five-count," Joe said slowly, much as a first grader would recite "Mary Had a Little Lamb." "Then I go downfield and try to get behind the ball carrier."

"Why do you hold for a five-count, Kotura?"

"Because I don't know if it's going to be a pass or a run," Joe said with increased confidence. "If the quarterback throws, it will be on four. So we wait until five to start downfield so we won't be penalized."

"You get a hundred, Joe," Mr. Zanoba declared. "And a bonus, too—you can carry one of the dummies all by yourself."

"Then I'll tote this one," Joe retorted with unexpected wit, grabbing Mark Chalmers by the shoulders.

Mr. Pearson smiled but squelched the laughter. The Riverside coaching staff allowed some foolishness both in the locker room and on the field, more than other high-school taskmasters, if Jim could believe what he heard.

"Mr. Snow will work out the ends and backs for extra time this morning," the coach continued. "I want both units running the new variation in scrimmage this after-noon."

Morning drills were given over mostly to "fundamentals" —blocking and tackling. Jim and Bill Baxter took turns at the dummy along with the rest. The quarterback or man under doubled as key blocker on one play series, the "power" pitches. Instead of handing off the ball, the man under pitched back, usually to his left halfback, but on the Rover counter or reverse, to the wingback. Then it was up to the quarterback to turn the opposing tackle or end, whichever bore inside.

Hackberry Jones did no better against the dummy than before. But Jim noticed that Mr. Zanoba wasted few words on the new recruit. And both Jones and Baxter were spared the one-on-one session. Instead they followed Mr. Snow to the sideline for separate instruction in throwing and receiving. The coach, observed Jim, talked to Baxter more than to Hackberry.

Then shortly, Jim and the other backs and ends were engaged in pass practice, too.

There were no new downfield patterns for this play—

only sideline, buttonhook and over center cut. It was up to the slot back himself to decide if he should go into motion and what pass pattern to run.

"We want you to take an end or a linebacker out with you," Mr. Snow told Chet Gordon and Ed Holloway. "If they will play outside of you to start with, good. Then don't go in motion. Your play depends on how they cover you. If it's a linebacker, go into motion and buttonhook. If it's a halfback and he is well out, then cut over center. Tell your quarterback how you are being played so he'll know where to look. Tell him if they double up on you. He can see for himself how they cover the split end, but he isn't even looking for you except as a third choice. All he'll know about your side of the field is what you tell him. Is that straight?"

Both Ed and Chet nodded.

Now Mr. Snow demanded the full attention of Rich Conover and Pat Wayne, the left halfbacks. "You are the safety valve," he explained. "You make one brush block and then go wide and slanting."

Rich Conover frowned and the backfield coach smiled. "I know, this is getting complicated. It has to be. This is really four plays in one. That's why we have to get the timing down pat. Let me give you the options and maybe you'll see your part in it more clearly.

"The quarterback's first choice is to run," he continued. "We're still the same Riverside team. Get this, Baxter and Carter—get it so firmly fixed in your minds that we don't have to go over it again. If you can see three yards, go! We don't flip the ball when we can go on the ground. Understand?"

Jim nodded, relieved. Then it was the same old quarterback option. It was his favorite play. He liked to cut in sharply and drive through a spread defense. With his weight and hitting low, he would pick up yardage unless hit behind the line of scrimmage. The much slighter Baxter could not do that.

"The second choice is to throw to the split end, either sideline or buttonhook." Mr. Snow hesitated, then added, "We'll throw to him a lot. We have to or this play won't work. We want two men covering him. Until that's done, the other options aren't much good. The split end will be Eudaly or Jones. Now, Jim—and you too, Baxter—we don't expect to complete *every* pass to the split end. Football would be child's play if that were possible. At least half of your throws will be to set-up plays rather than to make yardage. Am I clear?"

Jim did not answer at once. He understood the coach, all right, but he was not pleased. Put the ball into the air with the receiver covered! He had been taught to "eat it" first, or to pull it to his chest and fight back to the scrimmage line if possible.

"What about interceptions?" he asked finally.

Mr. Snow's lips twitched. "We don't want any," he said calmly. "I didn't say throw off balance, Carter, or anything like that. But we want enough throwing to this split end for the opposing secondary to start scrambling around the instant he lines up wide. Let's see—in an eight-minute quarter, if we are going pretty well, we can expect to run fifteen or sixteen plays. We're going to get moving quicker this year. I'd say that at least four of those plays will be passes to or toward the split end."

Jim took a deep breath and looked out across the field. So the scarecrow who just popped up, this human string-bean who had never played a down of competitive foot-ball—Hackberry Jones would be one-fourth of the River-side offense! And it would be Jones at split end rather than Dick Eudaly, Jim was sure of that. None of this split-end business had come up until Hackberry had joined the var-sity.

"But back to the options," Mr. Snow continued briskly. "Now listen, you two quarterbacks. The difference between a so-so quarterback and a star is his choice of options. That may be what makes Bart Starr the most effective passer in football, because he nearly always makes the right choice.

"First, you run. Second, you throw to the split end. Third, you turn and slot back. And fourth, you flip to your safety valve." The backfield coach hesitated, then chuckled softly. "The fifth choice—we send out three teammates and a stretcher."

Jim blurted out the obvious question without hesita-tion. "Who is going to be blocking for us all that time?"

"I wish you hadn't asked that, Jim," Mr. Snow said softly. A twinkle came into his eyes. "Of course, I see why you thought of it. It's your hide." Both hands came up in a gesture that looked almost like helplessness.

"You brought up something that the average spectator

and the girls in the pep squad may not even know," he explained. "A good passing team is a great blocking team. And protecting the passer, especially on this scramble sort of play, is the most difficult blocking assignment in football." The young mentor smiled. "I'm not selling you short, Jim, or Baxter, either. A good passing quarterback is important. He has a bunch of decisions to make under pressure and then must throw under pressure. But, believe it or not, a satisfactory passer is the easiest part of this puzzle to solve. More unusual, especially in high-school football, is the fine receiver any passer must have. That carries on into college, too. Take Baylor, for instance, where I went to conquer the world. We had *four* quarterbacks but only two real pass receivers."

He shrugged his shoulders. "But more important than either—and the hardest to develop—are the protecting linemen. If Mr. Zanoba didn't feel that he has the makings of an unusually good line, we wouldn't even try this play. And we're certainly not going to depend too much on this offense until we're sure that our line can muster up."

Mr. Snow gestured for the football. "But enough yakking," he said cheerfully. "Our job is to throw and catch the ball." He gestured toward the other end of the field. "Mr. Zanoba had his problems and he is working on them right now. Bill, you and Jim take turns throwing."

Jim frowned. Shouldn't it be "Jim, you and Bill take turns"? Surely this skinny sophomore wasn't moving in on the quarterback's job the way Hackberry was taking over split end!

It didn't take much of this throwing to increase his concern. These had to be running passes. Oh, the quarterback could stop suddenly and set his feet, but he had to be quick about it. And there was no use in Jim Carter's kidding himself. He couldn't whip the ball off his right ear on the dead run, not the way Baxter could.

Then, too, Rich Conover was throwing, and Rich was also better than Jim. Conover should be, of course; he had practiced running passes for several years. He had thrown some out of the left half position in junior high school.

But, Jim noticed, Rich could not connect with Hackberry Jones. He said with obvious conviction that it was not his fault.

"I can't tell what Jones is going to do next," he complained to Mr. Snow. "If I lead him one way, he's going the other."

"I know," nodded the backfield coach. "Jones isn't easy to get used to. But I have to point out that Baxter is learning, too, Rich."

Mr. Snow was right, conceded Jim, and he was glad that he had not complained. He felt the same way Conover did. How could you aim at a receiver who never was where you expected him to be? Yet Jim and Rich had only to stand back and watch to see that it could be done. Bill Baxter was doing it!

Rich must have been thinking the same thing. "How do you tell which way he's going to cut?" Rich demanded of Baxter.

The slight sophomore smiled. "I don't," he confessed.

"I just throw the ball and let him worry about getting to it."

Bill seemed reluctant to say more. As a first-year player he shouldn't be telling these two veterans anything, much less when others could hear him.

"And somehow he gets to 'em," he added. "I never saw anything like him."

"Who did?" Rich asked, an edge to his voice. "But I'll have to admit, he can catch passes—behind him, low, high, diving forward."

"Even falling forward or backward," Jim added. "It seems to me that he does better off balance than when the ball comes right to him."

The other receivers showed up well, too. Jim appreciated the grim expressions of Mutt Allison, Mark Chalmers, and Dick Eudaly, especially Eudaly. Dick was a senior, too. He had been an offensive starter the season before. Both Allison and Chalmers had lettered as ends. They had expected to share about equally the offensive end responsibilities, with Dick showing some edge. And here one of them was sure to be sidelined by this—this long-legged cowboy. Which end would it be? Left end? Jim shook his head. Would Mr. Pearson bench Dick Eudaly, his best blocking end, to put this freak into the lineup?

Coach Pearson would. He did that afternoon. From now on, the wingmen would be divided into "wide" and "tight" ends. Dick and Hackberry were the "wide" ends, of course.

The formation would always be the split end, slot back when Jones was on the field, the coach explained.

Of course, Jim fumed to himself. Jones couldn't block. Jones didn't even know the plays. He was only good for dipping down for a pass and leaping around like—like a goat! When Eudaly was in there, the Rovers could play solid football. And Jim was pleased that Dick was in the huddle with them for the first scrimmage plays.

"Let's show the coach something," Jim told his teammates. "We'd better, or some of us will be sitting out this season."

His cohorts responded. Mike Geary went for seven. Gordon made it a first down on the short counter. Geary ripped forward for five. Jim called for the power pitch. He took the handoff from Bob Crawford, whirled and lobbed back to Rich Conover. Then, driving hard, Jim collided with the defensive tackle allowed to come in. This, and Dick Eudaly's assignment, were the key blocks on this play. If Eudaly turned in the defensive end——

He must have. For as Jim scrambled to his feet he saw that Rich was fighting off tacklers well downfield. Mr. Snow blew the play to a stop and Jim looked toward the line markers. Fifteen yards!

Now they were moving. He told his teammates so. If they clicked like this, why risk a sophomore quarterback and a creature like Hackberry Jones!

Geary went for three and Gordon for four on the crisscross. The power pitch was played again—Jim believed it the ideal third down call. Again he and Eudaly threw the blocks which let Conover cut in. The defensive secondary was up fast but Rich could fight for that extra yard. He could do that almost as well as Jim Carter. Another first down.

Mr. Snow came into the huddle. Try the split-end plays, he urged. Jim obeyed, of course. Dick Eudaly went wide and Gordon moved into the slot-back position. Jim took the ball and swung to his left and——

Eudaly was covered. The defense was moving out except for the pursuit. Jim cut sharply and fought through clutching arms for a 2-yard advance. He rose ready to defend his option, but Mr. Snow offered only mild praise instead of criticism.

The same play? Why, Jim wanted to ask. They had been driving downfield like champions. Such a sustained march was uncommon in scrimmage, with the defensive players knowing the plays as well as the team with the ball. But Jim obeyed instructions. He even tried to throw. Not to Eudaly, for the split end was guarded closely by Ed Hollo-way. Jim looked to see if Gordon was over center and there the slot back was. But the pass was blocked by charging linemen.

"That's all right, Jim," approved Coach Snow. "It's like we said this morning—the blockers have to deliver or we look like shoeclerks. Give them time, though. Now you're on your own."

Jim took a moment to decide what to call. Third and eight. He called the power pitch again, this time the re-verse to Chet Gordon. But the opposing linebackers were blitzing, all four of them. Gordon did not get back to the scrimmage line.

The second offensive unit was given a chance with the ball then, but not before Coach Pearson had a few kind words for the varsity.

"You were moving fine," he told them. "The split-end plays fouled you up. Watch the second team work those patterns. They've had more practice."

That was true. But the main thing, and it hurt to admit it, was that the second unit had Hackberry Jones at the wide end post. And Billy Baxter was throwing. Billy could get rid of the ball quicker than he could, Jim had to admit. It seemed that the sophomore could take two or three steps and fire—and throw effectively. It appeared to Jim that Baxter was not throwing too accurately, that all the substitute did was to fire in Hackberry's direction. But Jones could leap to his right or left or straight up in the air and pull the ball down.

There were four straight completions. Then Baxter suddenly turned his attention to Ed Holloway, his slot back. Ed was wide open over center. The ball streaked right into his waiting hands. And the second unit had moved the ball to the 10-yard stripe.

Mr. Zanoba called for a break to adjust his defense. Rich Conover was assigned to cover Jones, too. Gordon would take the end outside, Conover in. The linebackers would blitz and——

Jim Carter sensed the play. It was no pass toward Hackberry Jones. Instead Bill Baxter was starting out wide.

No, Pete Miller had the ball. The fullback draw. It had been in the Riverside repertory all along, of course. All Baxter had to do was call it. Jim Carter used the play frequently himself.

But it had never worked like this for him. Golly, golly—there was nothing to it! Pete was across the goal line before any defender knew what was going on. Jim Carter ducked his head. He had never seen smoother ball handling by any quarterback. Had Bill decided on the play himself? If so, it must be described as a perfect call.

Yes, Baxter was responsible for the strategy. For Mr. Snow's voice rang out loud and clear.

"Billy boy, I love you. I could hug you. That's the prettiest play we've had in scrimmage yet."

The key linemen came in for praise, too. None of them had tipped off the play, Mr. Snow declared.

"What made you think of that play?" the assistant coach asked.

Young, smooth-cheeked Bill Baxter was actually blushing.

"Well, I guessed what the defense would do," he said. "Mr. Zanoba—he sure likes that blitz."

Now Jim was given his chance to work with Hackberry at left end. He tried passing to the new recruit and found it easier than he had expected. A high lob was almost sure to end up in Jones's hands. But defense coach Zanoba voiced a complaint after Hackberry's third reception. The end, he said, was guilty of pass interference. Mr. Pearson agreed.

"Jones, you can't use that elbow against the defender," the head coach pointed out. "Do you understand what interference is?"

Hackberry did not, except as far as it concerned the defensive player.

The unhappy Chet Gordon agreed that the Jones elbow was a most effective weapon.

"He gives it to you in the side just as he starts up," the halfback told Jim. Chet rubbed his bruised rib. "It's just like playing basketball."

Mr. Snow joined in the lecture, illustrating his point with Hackberry as the defensive halfback.

"I sure didn't know I was doing anything like that," Jones said apologetically.

"Of course you didn't," Mr. Snow told him good-humoredly. He slapped the recruit's shoulder. "We'll work on it, Hack. Don't let it bother you."

Jim Carter winced. So the special treatment for Mr. Hackberry Jones was going on and on! Why didn't the lanky boy have to take laps for rule violations as others on the squad did?

Then, as if adding insult to injury, there was Joan on the telephone that very night.

"Jim, I just saw Bob Crawford at the drugstore," she said excitedly. "He tells me that Hackberry has cinched a first-team position already. Is that true?"

"He worked some with the first team this afternoon," Jim hedged.

How could Bob know which was the first team and which the second unit?

"Oh, I'm so thrilled! Will you scrimmage again tomorrow afternoon?"

Jim answered as best he could. "I suppose so."

"Then I'm coming out to watch," declared Joan, "and I'll make Lucy and Beth come with me."

After the conversation was concluded, Jim stared at the silent receiver. Then he rose slowly and stiffly, and made his way to bed. He dreamed that night of a scrimmage session before a packed stadium, and all of them girls.

5

FROM BAD TO
WORSE

◆ ◆ ◆

The defensive drill was cut short that Thursday morning, at least for the offensive ends and backs. Nearly half an hour was given to passing drill. Mr. Pearson gave them four new pass patterns. Apparently he had decided to mix spread formation plays with his Regular T formation. Split the left end, send the right half in motion. The new strategy should not be difficult to learn, Coach Pearson explained as the backs and ends quickly ran through the new patterns.

It was not difficult. The complication was Jim's uncertain passing, especially to Hackberry Jones. He connected with Jones successfully some of the time, but not nearly as skillfully as Baxter.

True to Joan's promise, she, Lucy and Beth were among

the scattered spectators at the Thursday afternoon practice. Coach Pearson instructed Jim to work on the new plays against the first-string defense; then he left for the press box to take notes, leaving Coaches Snow and Zanoba to direct the scrimmage. Although Dick Eudaly began the scrimmage at starting left end, Hackberry replaced him after four plays at Mr. Snow's signal. The three girls' squeals of delight were audible to Jim on the field. He grimaced.

Three days of practice and already Hackberry was a first-stringer! Football should not be that easy, brooded Jim, as he watched Mr. Zanoba adjust the defense to counter the expected spread formation. Jim's offense had done well on the first series, making nine yards on a power sweep led by Jim and powerful Sandy Stone, the pulling guard. Why change a winning game, and why pass when you are running for first downs?

Jim then began scolding himself for his feelings about Jones. Joan was right. It was jealousy, pure and simple. As co-captain he should be happy that Jones might help the team. Still, thought Jim, as he led his team into the huddle, anybody who had worked as hard as he had for two long seasons would resent a newcomer who just strolled in and changed everything.

Somewhat to Jim's surprise, the new formation made a quick difference. With Jones split wide to the left and Chet Gordon in motion, the linebackers and halfbacks had to spread out. Mike Geary broke for twelve yards on a simple counterplay, then Rich Conover made eight on a halfback dive. The offense moved quickly downfield, even against Coach Zanoba's tricky defense.

With the ball at midfield, Jim called the power sweep out of the spread, then was overruled by Coach Snow. "Throw a pass, Jim," he ordered. "If we can keep the defense spread, we'll win some ball games, but you have to keep the linebackers and halfbacks worried about a pass."

Jim obeyed, despite his misgivings about his own ability. He called a look-in to Jones, and completed it right through the arms of the blitzing linebacker. The play gained eight yards even though Hackberry seemed to surrender and fall down when he was hit by halfback Steve Goodman. Dick Eudaly, thought Jim, would have broken free of that tackle and really made some yards.

Jim overthrew Hackberry on a longer sideline pattern, then completed another look-in, good for six yards.

"Good one, Hack," Jim said as they lined up again. "I threw too low that time."

"I don't mind diving for 'em," Hack returned good-naturedly.

A dive play gained the Red team a first down, and Coach Snow ordered another pass, the sideline pattern again. Jim looked for Hackberry on the left sideline, but couldn't find him—big Doug Prewitt was rushing from the left with arms high. Jim sidestepped Prewitt, then threw over the middle to Conover. Only fleet Steve Goodman prevented a touchdown, hauling Conover down from behind on the 18.

"That was luck," Jim told Rich as they met on the

scrimmage line. "I caught Wilson blitzing, and you were wide open."

The next play saw the crimson-clad team complete its drive. Jim called the power sweep to the left. He pitched back to Conover, then blocked both a linebacker and a guard who had diagnosed the play. Conover cut to the inside and streaked across the goal without a hand laid on him.

"Beautiful!" beamed Mr. Snow. "You see, Jim? With Jones pulling the halfback out, this team can go. That's the best drive I've seen all year!"

"Gee," muttered Jim as he knelt with Mike Geary and Rich for a water break, "Jones runs out there by himself and does nothing but get credit for the touchdown!"

"I guess he didn't see your double block," Mike put in. "Old Hack just looks so pretty running around like a goat! Some people just can't take their eyes off him."

"Don't worry, Jim," Rich told him. "I know how I got to the goal line. Our young friend Billy would never have blocked Billings and Prewitt. You're still *my* number one quarterback."

"That may not be enough," Jim said dismally as Mr. Snow's whistle ended the break and the weary offense took over again.

Jim beamed as Dick Eudaly rejoined the Red team, then scowled as the three girls cheered Hackberry Jones's return to the bench. A counterplay made twelve yards, with Eudaly delivering a brutal block on halfback Steve Goodman. Surely, thought Jim, the coaches will realize that it takes blocking to win football games. The Red made several first downs, mostly by running, although Jim did hit Eudaly with a look-in pass that gained fourteen yards.

"Good running, Dick," Jim complimented him in the huddle.

"Hmph," was Dick's answer. Then he muttered, "I'd better be doing something right. Your girlfriend's hero has just about put me on the bench." His voice was bitter.

The next play was not that "something right." The look-in fell incomplete.

"Sorry, Dick," Jim said to him. "It was low." But not that low, he was thinking; Hackberry would have caught it. And, to be honest, he knew Baxter would have completed the pass, even to Eudaly. There had been plenty of time. There was just no excuse for throwing badly at a distance of less than ten yards.

Apparently Coach Snow had about the same thoughts, for he motioned Jones and Baxter into the game, together with Pat Wayne and Ed Holloway at the halfbacks. The four replaced seniors trotted to the bench together.

Jim glanced toward the stands where the three girls were sitting. "They're sure quiet now," he told Rich. "Not like when Hack came out."

Rich did not answer, but sat glumly watching the play on the field.

What he and the others saw there made the seniors feel even worse. On the first play Baxter made a perfect running pass to Jones on the sideline, which was good for almost twenty yards. Then Baxter passed quickly to Holloway over the middle, and the fleet Ed outran safety Don Wilson to the goal line.

Coach Snow finally called the scrimmage to a halt, but not until Baxter had completed several more passes. Mr. Snow was beaming as he walked toward the locker room, making Jim feel all the worse. Golly, he thought, we scored twice and I completed passes all afternoon, and Mr. Snow's happy about Baxter. Even Mr. Zanoba looked jubilant, despite the touchdowns scored against his defense.

Jim overheard Mr. Zanoba mention the better blocking out of the spread; the passer hadn't been trapped once, even though the linebackers had been blitzing. He had to bite his lips to keep from retorting, "Yeah, but what about blocking on the running plays? Baxter's too small to block and Jones *won't*."

Friday's practice was more of the same. In the morning they concentrated on blocking and tackling, then came scrimmage that afternoon. After two hours of scrimmage in the September heat, the boys were almost too tired to talk in the locker room. Jim and Dick Eudaly were plainly unhappy—Baxter had again completed most of his passes to Jones, and Jim simply could not complete anything any longer than short look-ins. Even worse, there were no compliments about Jim's and Dick's blocking, and Mr. Snow was grinning from ear to ear every time Baxter passed to Jones.

On Saturday the scrimmage was cut short, and Jim and Bill Baxter joined the ends and halfbacks for more passing drills. Mr. Snow explained to Jim that he was taking too long to throw.

"You must be quick," he told the senior quarterback. "The receiver will be open only for a split second, and then the halfbacks will move in. You have to throw it before they react."

Jim tried manfully, but he seemed to pass worse when he tried to rush himself. Baxter, on the other hand, could throw well almost without looking, and seemed to have the knack of hitting the end just as he cut. Jim had several passes intercepted after the defensive backfieldmen joined the drill. They seemed to sense where he was going to throw the ball and move in front of the receiver.

Jim threw three straight incomplete passes to Dick Eudaly. One should have been caught. Dick returned to the huddle, muttering to himself.

"We ought to try Ping-Pong," Jim said, watching Baxter throw a perfect strike to Ed Holloway.

"Yeah," retorted Dick, "or else start playing football again, where ends have to block."

"If we could do that, I might know where I am again." Jim's voice fell. "I was first-string quarterback a week ago, and now I don't know what I am."

He was glad when Mr. Pearson blew the whistle to end the practice. Running his laps, he did not even bother to kid with Joe Kotura. The same old gloomy thoughts kept plaguing him—"I'm doing the best I can, and I just get further behind every day."

❖   ❖   ❖

Jim did not confide his worries about his place on the team to his parents. He was sorry he had said what he did to Dick and resolved not to mention the recent developments in such a way again. Publicly—to his teammates, his parents, Riverside students—he would report that everything was fine, that prospects looked good, that Hackberry Jones was learning fast and was quite a pass reciever.

But the prospect of listening to the "discoverers" of the new addition to the Rover squad brag about their accomplishment for another evening was different. Before he, Rich and Mike picked the girls up for their Saturday night triple-date, they made a firm agreement to cut off the usual raves about Hackberry the very minute the girls got started. Each would deliver the ultimatum to his own date; they would stand together to see that the subject of Hackberry Jones would not be discussed.

The plan worked fairly well until after the movie, when they stopped at the Snack Shack for hamburgers and soft drinks. Then, inevitably, the subject of football came up. It was Joan who first mentioned that Riverside's chances for the title seemed to be getting better every day. All agreed, and the matter could have ended there. But Joan had to add one comment, that it did look as if Hackberry Jones personally was responsible for the improvement.

"Hmph!" snorted Mike Geary. "What about Rich? He's gained more yardage in scrimmage this week than Hackberry and his fancy passes have—even when he's dividing time with Ed."

"Oh, Hackberry's valuable, all right," Jim put in, hoping to close the subject by agreeing with Joan. "But," he went on, "he doesn't do much but catch passes—some of the time. He doesn't block, and I'll bet Joan could tackle with more authority than he does."

Mike and Rich nodded agreement. They said nothing, however, as Jim gave them a warning look and a rather shamefaced "gosh, I've done it again" shrug of his shoulders.

Joan's eyes blazed. "You three are just plain jealous," she snapped. " 'He doesn't do much,' and 'He doesn't block!' You can't even see how much better the whole team looks. All you can think about is that Hackberry is getting more attention than you do!"

"Oh, for Pete's sake, Joan," Jim said impatiently. "Jealous of that clown? You must be out of your mind. Why should anybody be jealous of *him*, of all things?"

"Maybe it isn't jealousy," Beth put in, "but something is sure wrong. Rich is impossible to get along with these days, and that Jim Carter scowl shines forth any time we mention Hackberry."

"All three of you ought to be ashamed." Lucy had to speak her piece, too. "You ought to be grateful to us for bringing that boy to the team. What's the matter with you? Would you rather be big shots on a losing team than let Hackberry get some credit for a good season?"

"You girls don't know what you're talking about," Rich snapped. "Why don't you worry about clothes and makeup and leave football to us?"

"All right. It's a waste of breath to talk to you three anyway," Joan said. "But we may be smarter than you think we are. And don't expect us—or anybody else—to feel sorry for you when Hackberry turns out to be the star of the team and you're just another three members of the squad."

With that dig, the subject of football was dropped and the three couples parted unusually early under a sort of armed truce.

The next Monday Jim had still another blow. He entered Miss Roberta Miller's English class and took his seat. A moment later Hackberry appeared in the door. He surveyed the room, then saw the empty seat at Jim's left. His eyes lighted up and he hurried to take the seat.

"Isn't this luck?" he said with a grin. "I know just one person in this class and I get the seat next to him."

"Some luck," Jim answered weakly. Inwardly he groaned. He had not bargained for this. Hackberry on the football field was more than enough for him. "Are you sure you're in the right English class?" he asked.

"Miss Miller, room 123," Hackberry read from a card signed by the counselor. "This is 123, Miss Miller, isn't it?"

"That's right," Jim told him. "But how could you be assigned to an advanced American literature class if this is your first year in high school?"

"I don't know about that," Hackberry told Jim almost sheepishly. "I talked to a couple of teachers who asked a bunch of questions, and then they gave me two separate examinations. That was last week. I didn't hear any more from anybody until this morning. Then Miss Long—she said she's a special counselor, whatever that is—called me in and talked a long time. She said she'd fixed it so I could graduate in two years instead of three. I sure didn't argue with that. I want to get out of high school and into Texas A. & M. just as fast as I can."

A. & M.? Jim was surprised. Somehow he had never even thought of Hackberry as wanting to attend college.

Of course he had such plans, Hack said. It was Mister Ed's idea at first, he admitted, that he should go to A. & M. and study range management, but now he was even more sold on the idea than Mister Ed. Of course, since he owned only ninety acres of land, he wasn't a ranchman yet. But his property was close to the city limits and he was sure he could trade it for a larger tract further out. Mister Ed said not to hurry about it, though, for suburban property rose more in value than rangeland.

Jim's eyes went wide. Did Hackberry actually own ninety acres of land?

Sure. His brother had bought it four years ago. And when Sam was killed—well, it became Hack's as the only heir. He had paid off the mortgage against it and now he and Mister Ed were feeding cattle as partners. There were only ten yearlings, but it was a start.

Jim nodded. It certainly was a start, especially for a seventeen-year-old orphan.

"But if you haven't had English since junior high school, how can you hope to pass Miss Miller's course?" Jim asked his new classmate, feeling honestly sorry for him. Miss Miller was the most exacting teacher on the Riverside faculty. Only the exceptional student dared to sign up for her elective course.

"Gosh, maybe that Miss Long did put me in the wrong class," Hack answered. "I guess I can work real hard—I sure don't want to fail anything."

Just then Miss Miller swept in and, with a quick apology for her unusual tardiness, started calling the roll. When she came to Hackberry Jones she repeated the name with a frown.

"Hackberry?" She looked toward the voice that answered and then said sternly, "Mr. Jones, I do not permit nicknames in my classroom."

"It's not a nickname, ma'am," Hackberry told her, with an embarrassed grin at the smiles and chuckles from other students in the class. His father and mother had been looking for work in the West Texas cotton fields, he explained. The truck in which they were traveling had broken down just as his mother's childbirth labor began. His father had pushed the truck out of the burning sun and into the shade of a hackberry tree. There Mrs. Jones had given birth to her son. And, in appreciation of the only comforting thing in the whole situation, his parents had named him Hackberry.

Jim could not decide whether to believe this story or not. Miss Miller must have felt the same way, for her forehead was wrinkled in a dubious frown as she entered the name in her book. Some thirty minutes later, apparently still doubtful, she again addressed the new student as Mr. Jones.

Then she lectured on the purpose and value of this course, stressing her conviction that the study of American literature should develop understanding and appreciation of the American heritage rather than emphasize only facts. She would not follow the text exactly, she said. Students would have freedom and latitude in their reading and theme assignments if they showed understanding and appreciation of the course. Then she asked the students what they expected to gain from a course in literature. What was American literature, anyhow?

When she came to Hackberry, he replied that he did not understand the question. She tossed her head impatiently. Did he have no idea at all about what he should read and know about the literature of his own country?

"Yes, ma'am," the redhead answered promptly. "I sure do. My paw laid the law down to us about that. We had to memorize the Lord's Prayer and the Twenty-third Psalm. We had to quote the beginning of the Declaration of Independence and understand the rest. And the Gettysburg Address, of course."

He paused, looking hesitantly around the quiet room. Jim would not meet Hack's eyes. The student talking so familiarly of the Bible and the great American documents certainly did not seem to have much in common with the beanpole who learned his athletic skills from billy goats. Who would ever have thought he could make Jim Carter look weak by comparison in English class, too?

When Miss Miller said nothing, Hack went on. "All the

verses of 'The Star-Spangled Banner' and 'America' and the Pledge of Allegiance—Paw made us learn those, too."

"And other reading, Mr. Jones?" Miss Miller asked quietly.

"Oh, that didn't matter much to Paw," Hack said. "But most of the novels and magazine stories you can find don't hold a candle to the stories in the Bible," he added.

Jim and some of the other students smiled at that. Their amusement, however, was cut short by Miss Miller's serious, thoughtful look at the new student. His answer was completely satisfactory, she said slowly. In fact, it was such an excellent answer that it would be the basis of their first outside reading assignment. They would read the selections Mr. Jones had mentioned. There would be a written examination Monday. Grades would be A's or zeroes.

And, since Mr. Jones already knew the material, he could choose his own reading assignment, any book in the school library.

Up went Hackberry's hand. "How much will one of them cost?" he asked.

This time there were a few giggles as Miss Miller explained that no fee was involved; he had only to check books out.

The hand again. Did she mean that he could get all the books he wanted to read for nothing? His face beamed at her affirmative answer. He sure was going to have fun in this course, he said.

Miss Miller smiled broadly—the first time Jim had ever seen her do so. He took a deep breath. That Hackberry

Jones! Did he come up smelling like a rose every time? He had just sauntered out and stepped right into a varsity uniform. Now he had Miss Miller eating out of his hand, too!

6

A VICTORY AND
SOUR GRAPES

◆-◆-◆

"Winston shouldn't be difficult," thought Jim Carter as he
lined up for the opening kickoff of the season the following Friday night. The *American*, while picking Riverside
only third in the district, had predicted that the Red Rovers would beat Winston by at least two touchdowns. Coach
Pearson had cautioned his team against overconfidence—it
wasn't that Winston could beat them, he warned, but that
they could beat themselves.

The head coach's forebodings proved correct. Rich Conover received the opening kickoff and was tackled hard at
the Riverside 20-yard line. Jim called a fullback dive and
Mike Geary was swamped under after making only two
yards. Rich Conover barely regained the line of scrimmage
on a halfback follow, and then Winston stopped the River-

side power sweep far short of a first down. The Winston Wildcats had a heavy line, and they obviously did not intend to lie down and play dead. Perhaps the Winston team had not read the *American*.

Jim punted to the Winston 40, and the Wildcats took over. Again three head-knocking running plays produced little gain and no excitement. Their fullback, Mike Martins, was a big, burly fellow, but the team as a whole was slow. Mr. Zanoba's defense had no trouble stopping them. Winston ran out of the Straight T formation, but with little deception. Riverside's scouting reports indicated that they had very little passing threat and no speedy outside runner.

"We'll hold 'em all night," Jim said to Rich as the offense ran back to the field to await Winston's fourth down punt. "If our linebackers can crash, they'll never run over us in the middle."

Jim and his cohorts took over on their own 30. Jim carried himself on the first play, and made three yards before being tackled by the Winston halfback. Even that short yardage was a struggle, though. The Wildcats were playing a six-man line, with the two linebackers rushing and the halfbacks up close.

"We've got to loosen them up," urged Mike Geary in the huddle. "We can't run against ten men on the line of scrimmage."

Mr. Pearson sent instructions to start throwing onto the field with tackle Clint Northington. Jim called the sideline pass, splitting Dick Eudaly wide to the left. The Wildcats seemed confused; their reports said Riverside used the Regular T formation, not a spread with a split end. However, the Wildcats did not alter their 6-2-2-1 defense. Jim took the snap and rolled out, looking for Eudaly. The end was wide open, but Jim underthrew him badly. The quarterback slapped his leg in disgust. "Gosh," he thought, "even a girl can throw a ball ten yards!"

Third and seven! Riverside lined up in the same spread formation, with Chet Gordon in motion to the left. Jim pitched to Conover and blocked the linebacker, who had red-dogged and almost caught him before he pitched out. Conover faked the left-handed pass, then lowered his head and charged. A more elusive runner might have broken free, with two blockers in front and only the Wildcat secondary between him and the wide open spaces. However, Conover was trapped about midfield. The Wildcat safety man brought him down at the Winston 38.

Winston quickly called time out to adjust their defenses and receive instructions about the new development. Jim wasn't as exuberant as Rich Conover, who was grinning broadly. That spread formation did work, anybody could see that. But Jim still had to admit that it would work even better with a quarterback who was a passing threat instead of a hard-nosed runner.

Winston recovered quickly from the long gain. And their defense showed little if any respect for Jim as a passer. The two ends did drop back to cover the flat zones, but the linebackers continued to rush and the halfbacks moved even closer. Obviously they had no fear of an all-the-way pass, not with Jim at quarterback.

Mike Geary made only three yards at left tackle, and the counterplay gained only two more. On third down, Jim attempted a look-in to Dick Eudaly, who had again split wide. The pass missed its mark, though it did seem to Jim that it could have been caught. Jim punted for the corner, hoping to put Winston deep in their own territory, but the ball bounced into the end zone, giving the Wildcats possession on the 20-yard line.

"You've got to open up," advised Mr. Snow as Jim returned to the bench. "Those guys are big and rough, and we can't just run over them."

Jim watched as the Red defense allowed one first down, then again stifled the Wildcat offense. So far, neither team had shown much scoring ability.

Jim called the power sweep again, but Rich Conover was stopped at the line of scrimmage, even after Jim had blocked the end. The Wildcats were still charging, he observed. If only he could connect on one! He called the look-in, but this time he did not even consider throwing to Dick Eudaly. Instead he watched Chester Gordon cutting down the middle. Gordon was open, but Jim again threw badly, behind his receiver. The Winston safety man easily slapped the ball down.

Facing third and ten, Jim had to call a pass even if his last effort had been poor. Again he had Dick Eudaly wide open on the sideline pattern, but Dick dropped the almost perfect throw.

As Jim dropped back to punt, he was hoping there were no college scouts in the stadium. "If there were," he thought, "they wouldn't even recommend Carter and Eudaly for a fraternity team!"

The clock moved on to the end of the first quarter and into the second period with the same three pile-ups and a punt by one team and then the other. It was dull, plodding football, with nothing to show for the effort but sweaty jerseys.

After a short gain on a dive play, the Red Rovers called time out. "We've got to get going," urged Jim, "or else we're going to have to start practicing basketball. We're just moving in the same place."

"It'll stay that way until you loosen up their defense," Sandy Stone pointed out. "They're all over us. On every play I block the guard, and then I'm looking at the line-backer and the halfback going past me."

"I guess you're right," Jim agreed, "but the passes aren't getting us anywhere, either."

Jim did call the sideline pass again, and he had his first completion of the night. Apparently the Winston coach had instructed his team to allow the short passes and stop the runs. Dick Eudaly got a first down on the 37 before being stopped.

But in the huddle Jim was not satisfied or pleased. "That was too close," he told his teammates. "That defensive end almost had it, and if he had held on, he could have scored. A no-score game is no time to throw the ball away, and golly, we almost did it."

On the next play Jim went back to the running game. Mike Geary was stopped on the dive as the Winston defense dug in. The power sweep failed again. Rich Conover couldn't gain with the defensive halfbacks meeting him at the line of scrimmage.

In came instructions from Mr. Pearson. "The sideline pass," substitute guard Sid Duncan told Jim. "Coach Snow says they're not even trying to stop passes."

Jim tried gamely. He was almost swarmed under by the Winston linebacker and tackle. His throw was hurried. Dick Eudaly dived for it, but could not hold on.

"Sorry, Jim," mourned Dick as they gathered in the huddle. "We're not helping each other a bit."

Jim did not reply, but went grimly back to punt again. He got his foot into it solidly. The Winston safety let it bounce rather than try to field it over his shoulder. The ball rolled dead on the Wildcat 5-yard line.

"How's that for kicking?" thought Jim as he returned to the bench. At least he could punt.

With only two minutes left in the half, Winston decided to open up. A substitute halfback went wide, catching end Frank Thomas by surprise. Down the sideline the Wildcat streaked.

But Billy Cox was there. His hard tackle brought the runner thudding down. "Fumble!" Jim shouted from the bench. The elusive ball bounced free all too close to the sideline marker. Steve Goodman fell on it on the 22, just barely in bounds.

The Riverside cheering section came to life with its noisiest roar of the night. "Go, Big Red! Go!"

Jim grabbed his helmet and rushed toward the field. But Mr. Pearson's voice stopped him.

"Baxter, Jones, Holloway, Wayne, and Miller," the coach barked. "You've got only two minutes. Get moving!"

Jim shook his head and sank to one knee at the end of the bench. A sophomore quarterback in the clutch! He hadn't expected that, despite Baxter's showing in practice. Mike Geary, Rich Conover, and Dick Eudaly were obviously just as disturbed. The four seniors knelt together to watch play resume.

Winston did not change its defense, even with the new quarterback and the short time remaining. Riverside lined up with the end split and Ed Holloway in motion.

Hackberry Jones cut sharply to the sidelines, leaving the defensive end several steps behind. The pass from Baxter came straight and hard. Jones was wide open. He must have realized it, for he cut inside instead of going out of bounds. The defensive halfback made a halfhearted dive at him, but was caught far out of position. Hackberry threw the safety man off stride with a convincing feint. The last Winston pursuer sprawled helplessly on the ground as the lanky redhead crossed the goal line.

Jim, Geary, Eudaly, Conover, and Gordon hurried out for the extra-point attempt. Billy Baxter, holding the taller Jones around the chest in a bear hug, was dancing up and down. Bill ignored the end's obvious embarrassment. The ovation for the two was thunderous. Jim winced. Even though it was deserved praise, it hurt.

The football sailed through the uprights, and Riverside led 7-0. Even over the crowd's roar, Jim could hear Joan's voice— "All you have to do is throw to Hackberry." It just wasn't right, he fumed to himself. "We struggle for an entire half and can't score, and then out prance Baxter and Jones and make it look easy. Joan—and lots of others—will be perfectly sure they were right."

The game ended 7-0. Winston showed no more offense in the second half. Jim and his senior backfield made lots of yardage, but could not penetrate the Wildcat 20. Mr. Pearson allowed them to play almost the entire second half, preferring to run out the clock with a ground game as long as Winston presented no scoring threat. Baxter and Jones played briefly, connecting with a 10-yard sideline pass, but then watched the remainder of the game from the bench.

Linebacker Billy Cox was injured late in the fourth quarter, apparently twisting a knee. Jim finished the game at linebacker as well as quarterback, making several assists and two tackles.

Jim told himself he had played well. He had averaged over 42 yards in his punts, better even than some college kickers. The Rovers had gained 221 yards on the ground, and Jim's blocking and ball handling was responsible for much of that. He had kicked the game's only extra point, and proven himself a better linebacker than the injured Billy Cox.

These comforting thoughts were somewhat jarred when he and Joan walked into the gymnasium for the victory dance that night. In the first place, Jim's entrance went almost unnoticed by the celebrants. And to make it even worse, the reason was that most of the crowd was gathered around Hackberry Jones. The circle of students, five or six deep, was chattering happily and obviously admiring the "hero" of the afternoon's game.

"Do we have to have him everywhere?" Jim muttered to Joan. "At football, in English class, and now even at the dance! Seems like he'd have to see to his horses or his billy goats or something, for a change."

"Oh, for heaven's sake, Jim," Joan said impatiently, and she swept toward her protégé. Her scowl for Jim turned quickly into a welcoming smile as Hack saw her and waved.

And, if Jim considered this a poor start for a victory celebration, he was right. For Hackberry was the star of the show despite his refusal to join in the usual high-school dancing. Joan, Beth, and Lucy just wouldn't be satisfied with running the football team, Jim brooded. No, they had to direct Hack's social life, too. Joan persuaded him to do "Put Your Little Foot" with her. Then Lucy claimed him for a schottische. After Beth had her turn with a polka, the three teamed up to persuade Hack to bring out his guitar.

The enthusiastic reception of his three hillbilly numbers brought Jim, Rich, and Mike together in one corner of the gym.

"What in the world comes over people when that string-bean comes around?" Jim asked.

"I don't understand it," Mike put in. "They don't like country music any more than I do. Why, Lucy almost breaks the push button on the car radio when KJHS starts one of those Nashville-type programs!"

"Yeah, but look at her now, and all the rest of them—patting their feet, clapping, squealing." Jim snorted disgustedly.

Rich Conover agreed with Jim. "That Jones could step in a mudhole and hit an oil well!"

The next morning, reading the sports section as he ate breakfast, Jim actually thought he was going to be sick. For who did the newspaper praise? Hackberry Jones, of course. "A lean and rather ungainly split end by the curious name of Hackberry Jones caught one forward pass Friday night at Jones Field. That was enough to give Riverside High a 7-0 victory over the Winston Wildcats.

"For, with an agility as unbelievable as his name, Jones turned a simple sideline pitch into a touchdown romp, the only score as the Red Rovers launched their season in rather unconvincing style . . ."

The sportswriter did mention Jim's name. There was a paragraph about him, praising his kicking and steadiness. But between the lines, if not in actual words, the game story said quite clearly that the Red Rovers had very little offense with Jim Carter at quarterback. And college scouts could read between the lines.

7

A BRIEF
REPRIEVE

◆―◆―◆

Monday's practice saw even more emphasis on the new spread formation. Mr. Snow added a new play, a run or pass option. The pattern called for the right half, Gordon or Holloway, to go into motion, Hackberry to break deep, and the halfback to cut back in. If the quarterback saw daylight, he ran, picking up a block from the wingback.

Jim learned the play, but without enthusiasm. Plainly this maneuver was designed for the benefit of Billy Baxter, not himself. Its success depended on the threat of a long pass to Jones, to lure the defensive halfback and safety far out of position.

Dexter was the next opponent, and favored to beat Riverside, according to the *American*. Moreover, this was a district game, with the Rovers hungry for revenge. The

Dexter Cougars had crushed Riverside's championship hopes early in the season the year before by defeating the Rovers 14-13.

Jim kicked off, and the Crimson defense throttled the Cougars on the first series of downs. With Billy Cox still on crutches, Jim was a linebacker. Dexter's punt into a strong wind was short, only to the Riverside 45. Jim quickly called the team into a huddle, but out came Baxter, Jones, and Holloway. Jim joined the disgruntled Chet Gordon and Dick Eudaly on the sidelines.

The Rovers lined up in the spread, with Holloway in motion from the slotback post. Baxter bobbled the snap, but quickly recovered, faded back, and rolled to his left. Jim saw Hackberry elude the defensive halfback and jumped to his feet, shouting, "There he is!"

The Cougar line swarmed toward Baxter. But the slight sophomore managed to sidestep the charge and get the ball away. His pass was short, and Hackberry had to turn back and come in for the pass. Almost instantly the Dexter safety overtook him. Though hit hard, Jones held onto the ball. He came down on the Cougar 20—a 35-yard gain on the first Rover play from scrimmage!

The Dexter defense called time out. Certainly they had not expected usually conservative Riverside to open the game with a bomb. In came substitutes from the bench.

Baxter called the same play again. This time Jones was double-teamed. Baxter took one look downfield, then was off running. Holloway dumped the Cougar linebacker. Baxter eluded the onrushing halfback with a nifty feint. On the bench, Jim could not help grinning at Hackberry's clumsy effort to block out the Dexter safety. Jones hadn't learned a thing in the hours at the blocking dummy. He went at the safety standing straight up, and was simply pushed aside. But he had gotten in the way, and that was all the swift Baxter needed. He cut inside the safety and was in the clear. The other Dexter halfback hit Baxter from behind on the 3, but their momentum carried both players into the end zone. Touchdown.

Jim converted the extra point. 7-0.

Again the Riverside defense held the Cougars, even though Dexter fullback Frank Boyd gained eleven yards outside tackle. Jim made the tackle himself, pursuing and catching Boyd from behind. "Way to hustle, Jim," shouted Mr. Zanoba from the bench. Defensive halfback Steve Goodman had been blocked out by the Dexter end, and Boyd might have gone all the way if Jim had not caught up with him.

The Cougars tried an end sweep on first down, but Mark Chalmers, the defensive end, turned him inside and held the play to a one-yard gain. A dive play gained another yard. On third down the Cougars elected to pass. Sandy Stone rushed hard, with Jim right behind him. Stone hit the passer high, and the ball bounced free. Jim pounced upon it. But the referee ruled the play an incomplete pass rather than a fumble.

Fourth down. This time the Dexter punter really got his foot into the ball. Safety Chester Gordon retreated, then let the ball drop rather than attempt to field it over his shoulder. It took a Dexter bounce and rolled to the Riverside 20 before being whistled dead.

Jim quickly called the huddle, then looked anxiously to the bench to see if he would be replaced. Instead, Mike Geary and Chet Gordon and the rest of the offensive team came out. Apparently Coach Pearson at least trusted Jim to hold onto the ball when the Rovers had a poor field position.

Mike brought instructions from the bench. "Try to work it downfield before you do anything fancy." Jim complied, calling the fullback follow. Geary plunged forward for almost seven yards before being stopped by the Dexter safety. The Riverside line was heavier than their Cougar opposites; Geary had a hole big enough to drive a truck through.

On second down Rich Conover hit the same hole on the crisscross and made five more yards, and Dexter called time out to adjust their defenses.

"Keep hitting, you guys," Jim urged. "We can score running and won't have to pass."

On first down, Jim called the straight dive. Rich Conover hurtled five yards through the big hole cleared by Sandy Stone.

But from the huddle, Jim noted a change in the Dexter defense. They were tightening up, moving the linebackers almost on the line of scrimmage and pulling the halfbacks in tightly.

He considered calling a pass, but decided to follow Mr. Pearson's instructions. Rich Conover was hit almost at the line of scrimmage on an off-tackle slant.

Third and five! In came Mark Chalmers at tight end with another message. "Pass across the middle," he told Jim. "Coach Snow says they're wide open with their linebackers so close."

Jim's pass was wobbly. But as Coach Snow had predicted, Dick Eudaly was wide open. The pass was so soft that a baby could have caught it. Eudaly gathered it in. He loped past midfield before being overhauled.

Eudaly ran back to the huddle clapping his hands. Jim was delighted, too. If the Rovers could run well enough to force the opposition into a tight defense, even he could pass for yardage.

Jim glanced toward the stands as the Riverside cheering section shouted, "Go, Big Red!" He'd show Joan and her friends that they could score with Hackberry Jones sitting on the bench.

First and ten. Jim called the wide pitchout. Maybe the defensive halfback would expect another pass. But if so, he was not impressed with Jim's passing, for he met Rich Conover almost at the line of scrimmage. The determined Rich plowed right over him for four more yards.

The inside reverse was Jim's second down call. It brought a gleam into Mike Geary's eyes. Mike had scored his first touchdown on that play, last season. It called for Jim to roll to his right, with the two halfbacks in front as if blocking for an end sweep. Jim would then hand off to fullback Geary, who hit back to his left. Hopefully the linebackers would be drawn out of position, leaving a hole.

But Dexter's linebackers were rushing too fast. Jim was

hit just as he handed off, and Geary lost his momentum trying to hold onto the ball. He was downed for a 3-yard loss.

Third and nine. This time left-handed Rich Conover took Jim's lateral and rolled to his left, looking for a receiver. Eudaly was tightly covered. Rich threw wide to avoid a big loss. Jim shook his head as he went back into punt formation. Dick just did not have Hackberry's ability to elude pass defenders. He had been tightly covered by only one defender, while Jones was usually wide open even when he was double-teamed.

The punt was good, down to the 15 and out of bounds. Unlike many college coaches, Mr. Pearson believed in the angled kicks. Even though he conceded that a sideline kick made punt returns more dangerous, he felt that the possibility of sticking the other team near its goal was worth the risk. There was nothing more demoralizing and dangerous, he argued, than to take the ball over inside the 10-yard line.

With less than a minute in the quarter, the Cougars wisely elected to play it safe and hold onto the ball. They ran two quarterback sneaks before the gun sounded to end the quarter, giving Dexter the advantage of the brisk September breeze.

Jim played the entire second quarter, on both offense and defense. With the wind at his back, the Cougar punter kept Riverside in their own territory, even though the Cougars could not manage a drive against the Crimson defense. Dexter got down to the 20 with less than a minute

left in the half, but Jim intercepted a poorly thrown pass
and ended the threat. Then he fell on the ball twice to run
out the clock.

"You fellows play as if you want to win," praised Mr.
Pearson in the locker room. "If you keep up that kind of
defense, we'll give some people fits this season."

Mr. Snow was less enthusiastic about the offense. He instructed Jim and Bill Baxter to try to score at least once in
the third quarter, when they would again have the wind
advantage.

"We've got to keep them opened up," he explained.
"They're moving into an eight-man line on us and getting
into our backfield. If we fumble, the game's tied up."

Jim did not argue, of course. But he did not agree. With
Riverside in the lead, he wanted to stay on the ground and
wear the Dexter line down. He did not believe Dexter
could keep on holding the Rovers, not after all the punishment their line was taking.

Jim kicked off to open the second half, and Frank Boyd
almost broke free again. Sandy Stone finally made the tackle, about midfield. But the Rover defense was determined.
Jim broke up a third down end sweep, preventing a first
down. Dexter kicked to the Riverside 27, where Rich made
a fair catch.

Two running plays netted five yards. Then Jim followed
Mr. Snow's instructions and opened up. Eudaly was open
on the sideline pass. But the ball slipped off the side of
Jim's hand and went incomplete.

Jim went grimly back to punt. He sailed it high and far,

down to the Cougar 30, where Mark Chalmers made the tackle. Dexter ran two off-tackle slants, then attempted their first long pass of the evening. Steve Goodman had the end well covered, and the pass hung in the wind. Steve came in two steps and grabbed the ball away from the intended receiver.

First and ten in Cougar territory. Jim's cohorts looked nervously toward the bench before joining the huddle. Coach Pearson was not ready to send in the sophomores and juniors, and waved them to go ahead.

"This may be our last chance," Jim advised his mates. "We've got to move now."

Two running plays produced a first down. But the Cougar defense quickly showed equal determination. Rich Conover was stopped cold on a follow play. The power sweep yielded only two yards.

Third and eight. Jim started to call the play in the huddle, but a tap on the shoulder stopped him. It was Bill Baxter. Jim, Ed, Rich, and Chet went to the bench.

"I'm glad to turn it over to them," Jim remarked as he wiped his sweaty face with a towel. "They make their passing click better than we do. And it's a good time to have the passing team in there."

"You're right about that," Rich agreed.

Baxter and Jones struck at once. The sideline pass to Jones was good for ten yards and a first down—even though the Cougars were expecting just that play. They chased Hack frantically, but they simply couldn't cover him. Besides, Baxter threw a perfect strike.

The juniors hit paydirt on the next play. Baxter rolled to his right, again looking for Jones on the sidelines. The Cougar halfbacks rushed over to guard Jones, and there was Ed Holloway all by himself. Baxter threw hard and straight, right across the middle. The ball hit Ed squarely in the chest. He held on and streaked twenty-five yards into the end zone. No defender came close to him.

Four passes, four completions, two touchdowns! It was easy for Jim to see why Pat Wayne and Pete Miller had replaced Geary and Chet Gordon. The juniors blocked better for the passer. Jim pointed this out to Mike and Chet, and they quickly agreed. And it was just as obvious why Holloway went in for Conover. Ed was a better receiver and more dependable with his blocks on the running plays. The wide formation called for scramble blocks rather than the usual variety. The juniors had just adapted more quickly to the new style.

That logic did not contribute to Jim's satisfaction or peace of mind about the way the season was going—at least for him. He could not forget that if it had not been for Joan and her insistence on bringing Hackberry Jones to Riverside, there would not be a new style.

Jim and the seniors played all the remaining game. They even scored, the first touchdown of the year for Jim's offense. Dick Eudaly was straining to show that he could play split end; Jim was determined to prove that he could pass. Twice he hit Eudaly on short look-ins. With the ball on the Dexter 40, he called the halfback pass from the reverse. Dexter was taken completely by surprise. Rich Conover's left-handed pass was straight and hard, although a little too high. Eudaly had to leap to catch it. As he came down, he lost his footing. But he stumbled desperately for the goal line. A desperate lunge by a defender threw him off stride at about the 10, and he was finally brought down on the 5. The demoralized Cougars hardly touched Mike Geary on the next play. Touchdown.

Jim converted his fourth straight extra point of the season, and time ran out without another serious threat by either team. The final score—21-0.

The Rovers spent more practice time on offense during the week before the St. Elmo game. Never before had they devoted so many hours to offense, Jim thought. It was probably because they were running two offenses instead of one. The Regular T and the running game were not neglected, but Mr. Snow kept adding plays out of the spread.

Hackberry had no trouble learning his simple assignments. He ran a pass pattern on every play, even the running plays. That made sense. If an end couldn't block but could catch passes—well, he could take out a defensive player in his own way. He had to be covered on every play, no doubt of that.

Coach Snow drilled Conover and Ed Holloway on deceptive motions. Chet Gordon and Mike Geary began to improve on their scrambling blocks. "Blockers have to think on this team," lectured Mr. Snow. "On drop-back passes, blocking is mainly getting in the way and holding. But when the quarterback rolls out, you have to roll with him. And you have to be ready to move out in front if he has to run."

Geary also proved a better safety valve than Pete Miller. Geary had been all-district last year as a running fullback. He was simply a better runner than his junior rival.

St. Elmo was a non-district opponent. Jim rather expected Mr. Pearson to order a conservative game, since the Rovers should have no trouble with the Cardinals. There was no use in showing the other district teams too much of the new Riverside offense. But Mr. Pearson surprised the quarterback by instructing him to throw the first time he got field position. "Hackberry is your primary target," he said. "Throw to him. We want the opposition to team up on him, assign two players against him. Then you'll have the wingback or tight end open over center. But don't throw there too much—that's where passes get intercepted. If you're in doubt, throw to the outside or run."

The right or tight end had become a receiver in the plays learned the week before. The wingback cut down and out or in, according to where Jones was going. Dick Eudaly had learned the signals for right end, though Mark Chalmers was proving a good receiver.

Jim started the game at linebacker, then took over at quarterback when St. Elmo punted. St. Elmo held the Rovers, but Jim let out on his punt, carrying it fifty-four yards. Riverside held, and took over on the punt at their 42-yard line.

That was good field position, so Jim opened up as he had

been instructed. He threw to Jones on the sidelines, but the pass was high and wide. His next attempt, to Conover on the opposite sideline, was too low.

Disgusted, he started to call a running play, but in came another pass pattern from Coach Snow.

Jim rolled to his right. A hard charge by both Cardinal linebackers forced him to give ground. Then he lobbed over the onrushing Cardinals to Mike Geary. The fullback was five yards behind the line of scrimmage, but he could run. He went outside and gained fifteen yards and a first down.

Jim hit Chalmers on the jump pass for eight yards, then called the draw play. He faked beautifully. The Cardinal linebacker and a guard knocked him off his feet, but not before he had handed off to Geary. When he got up, Geary had made another first down, on the St. Elmo 22.

Jim called the look-in, scarcely believing his team's quick success. He threw it perfectly to Hackberry Jones. Instead of falling down, Jones dodged an onrushing Cardinal halfback and went in for the score. Jim converted, and Riverside had a 7-0 lead.

The quarter ended after another exchange of punts. Baxter, Wayne, Holloway, and Miller took over the Crimson backfield. Jim sank wearily down on the bench.

Baxter started off in a hurry. First he hit Jones on a look-in, then Holloway across the middle. He rolled out again, looking for Jones on a deep pattern. The St. Elmo linebackers were all over him, but he reversed the field and broke free. The pint-sized boy could run. He got to the sidelines and fairly flew. Fifty-four yards later he stood panting in the end zone, and the Riverside fans went wild.

14-0 at the half. Mr. Pearson expressed his pleasure in no uncertain terms. Jim was happy himself. After all, he had completed four of six passes, one for a touchdown, and had moved the ball well. Besides that, he thought, he was showing up well on defense. The Cardinals had made precious few yards through his linebacker position.

Jim took over the offense again to open the second half. He completed another good pass, this time for eighteen yards, but Rich Conover's fumble stopped the first Rover drive. They took over again several minutes later, but on their own fifteen.

It was no place for passing. Jim called the fullback sweep. Mike Geary made nine yards, and Jim made the first down himself on the quarterback sneak. But St. Elmo tightened up, forcing Jim to kick after three running attempts.

Riverside took over again late in the quarter, after St. Elmo fumbled on the Riverside 40. Jim had caused the fumble. He met the Cardinal ball carrier head-on and knocked the ball loose. Bud Jameson fell on it, and the Crimson offense was back in business.

Chet Gordon made five on the inside reverse, then in came substitutes—Baxter, Holloway, Wayne, and Miller. Bill Baxter promptly found St. Elmo with only single coverage on Hackberry Jones. He completed three straight passes to the end. The end of the quarter interrupted this pattern.

A long pass went to Holloway over the middle, and

Riverside had a first on the St. Elmo 5. Jim recognized the next play immediately, the run or pass option. Bill cut wide and seemed to have running room, but he chose to throw instead—to Hackberry, of course. He simply lobbed the ball over the head of the defensive halfback, who had rushed up to prevent the run. Hackberry gathered it in right off the shoulder of another defender. Third touchdown.

Jim converted again. He hadn't missed a point after touchdown all year, and did not intend to. Riverside had lost two games the previous season by the margin of a single point. Those hurt.

21-0. Now Mr. Pearson called in the ragnots. The starters didn't play another down. Jim sat on the end of the bench and watched the game and the Riverside cheerleaders in perfect contentment.

The Rovers had completely dominated the game. With their defense, and the offensive spark generated by the spread formation, Jim could think of no reason for Riverside not to be championship material.

Mr. Pearson evidently had the same idea, for he practiced the Rovers long and hard the following week. Travis, their next opponent, was another non-district game, the last one for Riverside. But the district had three unbeaten teams—co-favorites McCallum and North Side, and "upstart" Riverside. That was the local paper's word for the Red Rovers.

"Coach Pearson plucked a brilliant split end out of the blue and is making the most of him. In fact, it is proper to describe the Red Rover attack as Hackberry Jones and company."

Jim groaned. Was that fair to him, Baxter, and the other hard-working Rovers?

Then Jim read on and no longer felt sorry for Bill.

"And pint-sized, slippery Bill Baxter is the other Rover surprise. Though only a sophomore, Baxter can pass; he can scramble; he is colorful. If Riverside is to go all the way, Jones and Baxter must do it. And fair warning to District 15—both have another year."

8

WHAT HAS THE
CAPTAIN DONE?

❖ ❖ ❖

That Saturday night Jim, Rich, and Mike and the three girls gathered at Beth's house for what proved to be a rather uncomfortable evening. The records they usually enjoyed were the same, Beth's special dip had its customary distinctive tang, but still the minutes dragged by. To Jim it seemed like walking on eggs as he clamped his mouth shut for about the twentieth time before mentioning football or anything that might bring up the name of Hackberry Jones. The others must have been suffering from the same constraint. There were too many long silences, the girls talked to each other too much, and the easy banter in which the six usually indulged never did get started.

Finally it was late enough so that Jim could suggest going home without seeming downright rude. But even that did not work out well. As soon as they were alone in the car Joan said, "Jim?" in a tone of voice that warned him something was coming.

"I've been thinking," she went on, when he had grunted a reply. "You know, Mother is getting worried about our going steady. I really wonder whether it is a good idea for us to go on dating so regularly, and not go out with other people."

"Why not?" Jim said shortly. "It suits me. How about you?"

"Oh, it suits me, too," Joan said quickly. "But oughtn't we to be mixing around more, knowing other people with other interests better? You know what Miss Miller always says—'Never pass up a chance to broaden your experience.' Maybe we both should try to broaden our experience."

"Miss Miller's pretty smart, I admit," Jim retorted, "but I don't quite see her qualifications to advise us about going steady."

"You don't need to be nasty. There might be a hundred reasons why she's an old maid."

"I'm not being nasty. But skip it. If you don't want to go with me, that is all right with me. I'll take you home right now, and I promise not to limit your experience anymore."

"You're not trying to understand what I'm saying, Jim Carter," Joan said, a tinge of anger in her voice. "I want to date you. I like to date you. You aren't 'limiting my experience'—not very much, that is. I just don't want to

keep on dating you or anybody else steadily. Isn't that completely sensible?"

"Okay, okay," Jim muttered. "Not steadily any more,
not at all if that's the way you want it."

"That's not the way I want it," Joan told him. "In fact,
I want a date with you tomorrow afternoon. Hack gave me
two tickets to the regular Sunday rodeo at Oak Hill. Will
you go with me?"

Jim did not answer at once. Hack, the hero on the football field—Hack, the hero in English class—Hack, the center of the stage at the dance—why should he give up Sunday afternoon for the prospect of seeing Hack play the
hero at still another activity?

"I don't think I can," he answered finally. "I'm sure I
can't get the car."

"No problem," Joan answered quickly. "We can go in
mine. My folks don't mind my using it for a daytime date."

"Okay then, I guess," he said. Immediately it dawned
on him that he had let Joan outmaneuver him again. What
did either one of them know or care about rodeos? The
only reason Joan wanted to go was to drool over Hackberry Jones.

The rodeo arena at Oak Hill, just southwest of Austin,
was not much. Of course Jim had no basis of comparison
but what he had seen on TV, but every kid baseball field
in town had better bleachers, Jim thought, as he and Joan
climbed into the unpainted, rather rickety stands. Everything was dusty and covered with the fine brown silt that

flew like shaken flour with each footstep. The arena was surrounded by a fence made of tin sheets leaning lopsidedly against cedar posts. Mister Ed's monthly rodeos, quite understandably, were not a paying proposition, Jim figured, but it did seem to him that the riding stables ought to make enough that the owner could make some improvements here. There were lots of nuts like Lucy, Beth, and Joan, to say nothing of university students, who spent money like water at the stables.

It was impossible not to notice Hack Jones. He seemed to be everywhere, busy with chores that Jim could only guess at, on horseback, on the ground, talking first to this person, then that, obviously respected by them all. Jim was instantly aware of the difference between the gawky beanpole in an ill-fitting football uniform, and the lithe, graceful "cowpoke" in bright plaid shirt and skin-tight jeans. Hack seemed at home, at ease. He definitely belonged in this atmosphere.

Another shocking difference showed up during the bronc riding. The instant a rider was thrown or one held the saddle past the 10-second time limit, up tore Hackberry to assist. He could grab reins and stop the bucking or pull a rider out of the saddle in seconds. It looked dangerous, very dangerous to Jim. Could that reckless young man in the tight jeans be the split end who avoided bodily contact in football, who blocked and tackled as if terrified of being hurt or hurting someone else? It didn't seem possible.

But Joan's constant "Oh, look at Hack! Isn't he wonderful? Did you see the smooth way he handled that wild,

rough horse?" made the truth all too obvious. It *was* the
same Hackberry Jones, no matter how different he appeared to be.

In the calf roping, Hack was the fifth of eight contestants. He charged out after a Hereford calf and threw his
loop almost at once. Down went the calf. More quickly
than Jim could follow the action, Hack was leaning over
the struggling animal, grabbing three legs. He made his
tie skillfully, and the handful of customers broke into applause when his time was announced—12.6 seconds.

Jim shook his head. "I don't know much about rodeos,"
he remarked to Joan, "but isn't that an unusually low
time?"

Joan nodded. "It certainly is," she told him. "It is good
even with these small, gentle calves. Hack usually posts a
time under fourteen seconds," she went on, "but he's won
his biggest prizes with even higher times. His times were
14.9 and 15.2 when he took day money two days in a row
at Cheyenne." Her face broke into a big smile. "Our friend
Hackberry is the youngest competitor ever to win first-day
money in a major rodeo," she said proudly.

Just then a voice came over the public address system.
Hackberry Jones had won first money.

Joan grabbed Jim and squealed with delight. Jim, in
turn, did not try very hard to conceal his "so what?" re-
sponse. But suddenly he started. Won first money! Cash
prizes! How could Hackberry accept cash prizes and still
be eligible for high-school athletic competition? There was
an absolute rule about prizes in the Texas Interscholastic

League—for golfers, Jim was sure. Hadn't Barry Scott been disqualified as a member of the Riverside golf team for accepting a set of matched irons won in a summer tournament? The limit was twenty-five dollars in cash or merchandise. Didn't the same rule apply to football players who were also rodeo performers?

"How much money does Hack win in contests like this?" he asked Joan, hoping he did not sound as excited as he felt.

"Oh, I don't know exactly," Joan answered innocently. "The stakes here are small, but those two big days at Cheyenne were worth one thousand dollars apiece. His two thousand dollars there bought that pickup truck he drives and paid his brother's funeral expenses."

Jim's pulse beat more rapidly. Unless the Texas Interscholastic League made an exception of rodeo winnings— and why should they—Hackberry Jones was ineligible for the Riverside football team!

As they drove home Jim hardly heard Joan's chattering about all of Hackberry's skills. His mind was racing with thoughts of a chance for a decided upswing in his football fate. Why had no one questioned the lanky newcomer's participation? Jim could answer that one for himself. It hadn't occurred to anyone. Who would ever even think of asking a seventeen-year-old boy if he had won any big money prizes in rodeos?

Let Hackberry go on drawing the applause of that small crowd at the Oak Hill arena and collecting his first money. Let the girls keep on raving about that *marvelous* Hackberry Jones. It did not matter now. Jim Carter and his Riverside teammates could go back to playing the kind of football they knew and were good at.

An early morning telephone call to the director of the Texas Interscholastic League at his Austin office confirmed Jim's suspicions. Certainly the twenty-five dollar limit on prizes in any sort of athletic competition applied to rodeos—golf, tennis, baseball, shuffleboard, or even Ping-Pong, if necessary. Of course, when a question arose the district committee would rule on individual eligibility, but the rule was quite definite and clear, and no exceptions were permitted.

As he returned to morning homeroom after making his call, Jim could hardly keep from chortling. All through first and second period classes he pretended attention, but could not shut off the thought of what the team would be without Hackberry Jones. Coach Pearson would undoubtedly go back to their old-style team, with an all-senior backfield and Dick Eudaly at left end. They could win without Jones and the razzle-dazzle built around him. Hadn't the Crimson defense stopped every opponent cold? Hadn't Jim Carter outkicked every rival? Golly, Jim exulted, it could still be the season he had dreamed of for nearly a year. He would be the key figure in the Rover offense as well as a bulwark on defense.

But, stopping in the hall to talk to Joan for a moment, Jim began to have other less welcome thoughts about the new turn of events. Joan wouldn't understand at all, he realized. Some other students wouldn't, either.

He would just have to forget about those who might criticize what he was doing, he decided, as he got a permit to go to see Coach Pearson during third period. After all, he was co-captain of the team. Such obvious ineligibility could not possibly be kept a secret all season. A responsible captain had an obligation to report anything that could so drastically affect season results. The Rovers simply couldn't challenge for the district championship and then have all their games forfeited.

What he was doing was certainly right and fully justified, Jim told himself. Still, he would ask Coach Pearson not to tell anyone where he had learned about Jones's probable ineligibility. Things would be a lot easier if he didn't have to try to make Joan understand.

"You did the right thing, Jim," Coach Pearson assured him when he had heard what his co-captain had to say. "I'm just glad I know about it before we play any more district games. If Jones is actually ineligible, we'll forfeit our game with Dexter. I'd hate to risk any more forfeits."

"That hurts our chances, doesn't it, Coach?" Jim asked quietly.

"Of course. But we still have an outside hope. Another forfeit would ruin us for good."

Jim was called out of his sixth period class. Mr. Pearson had talked to Hackberry. The red-haired youth admitted that he had accepted every money prize due him. Principal Robbins had turned the matter over to the district committee, with a request for a prompt hearing. There was virtually no doubt of what their ruling would be. Meanwhile Jones was off the squad. He could not practice or play again.

"You won't bring my name into it when you tell the squad, will you, Coach?" Jim asked as he was dismissed.

"Of course not," the coach answered, "though it really doesn't matter. The facts would have come out sooner or later anyway. You should have told me. You did. So that is that."

"My girl wouldn't see it that way," Jim explained lamely. "I sure don't want to have to convince her I was right."

"All right, Jim. I don't have to say where I got this information, and I won't."

Coach Pearson told the squad what had happened that afternoon right after calisthenics. He told it simply. The district committee would, he was sure, rule that Jones had to be considered a professional athlete. The Rovers could consider that their season record already listed one loss. Now they had to get down to work and try to recover from this stunning blow.

Watching his teammates' faces as the coach talked to them, Jim could see little reaction other than shock. He did meet Dick Eudaly's eyes. Dick seemed surprised, but there was also a hint of a smile. Billy Baxter looked distressed, and well he might. Without Hackberry, Billy just might not be in the quarterback slot so often or so long. Now young Baxter could get his share of "waiting till next year."

"Who will the girls rave about now, I wonder," Rich remarked as they trotted onto the field for the practice session.

"Maybe you and me for a change," Jim said, but without much conviction.

"Maybe so—if they can stop crying long enough. Joan is going to take this hard, Jim. Hack has been her baby, you know."

"I sure do know. I haven't heard anything else all season," Jim said. He was glad to hear the coach's whistle. Talking about what had happened made him nervous.

The practice session saw Eudaly back at split end. Apparently the coaches did not intend to scrap the formation and the plays developed around it, even if they no longer had Hackberry Jones in the lineup.

The difference between Dick Eudaly and Hackberry at the split-end post was readily apparent, even to Jim, who was desperately trying to make Dick look good so that the team would not be demoralized by the loss of Hackberry. Even the ragnot defense had little trouble covering Dick. Twice Jim was thrown for losses when he couldn't find an open receiver.

Mr. Pearson had scheduled only thirty minutes of scrimmage, and Jim urged his offensive team to score quickly. "We've got to move, men. If we can't run over the ragnots, the team will think we can't score at all, and we'll lose our confidence. Let's go!"

In spite of Jim's urging they scored only once, and were stopped cold when Mr. Zanoba ran in the regular defense against them. Jim had expected the running plays to work better with Dick instead of Hackberry at split end—after all, Dick was clearly the better blocker. But it didn't work that way at all, to Jim's concern. The defensive halfbacks didn't worry much about covering Dick on pass patterns, especially not with Jim at quarterback. Instead they played the ball carrier, often meeting Rich and Mike right at the line of scrimmage.

Mr. Snow was openly critical of the offense. "You guys couldn't beat an egg," he snapped after a disappointing series. "We've given you seven downs instead of four, and you still haven't made ten yards for a first down."

Jim was resentful and defensive. "How can we?" he snapped. "They know all our plays, and the halfbacks are acting like tackles. Blocking assignments can't work when there are eleven men on the line."

"You're supposed to move them off the line, or pass over them," Mr. Snow shot back. "There's no rule in football that the defense has to play where the offensive quarterback wants them to."

Jim tried to pass more often, but wasn't successful. He was relieved when Mr. Pearson ended the scrimmage, and worried as he took his shower.

Rich and Chet shared Jim's concern as the three walked home after practice. "Golly," moaned Jim, "we couldn't move the ball at all today, not even against the ragnots. I sure thought we would have a better offense with Dick in there, at least on running plays."

"We've just got to face it," Chet answered glumly. "As

sorry as Jones was most of the time, he made the offense
work. You just had to stay with him, because he could run
like the wind, and he could catch any pass thrown."

Jim went to his room immediately after supper and
spent several hours in deep thought, pretending to study
in case his mother walked in. What had he done to the
Riverside team? He had honestly thought that they would
be just about as good without Hackberry—their running attack surely wasn't as bad as it looked today in scrimmage.

However hard he tried, Jim couldn't convince himself.
He finally fell into a restless sleep that night fully realizing
what Coaches Snow and Pearson had obviously known all
along—without Hackberry Jones, Riverside had a mediocre
offense and a fair defense, and no more. Only with Jones
at split end and an explosive offense from the spread formation would Riverside have any possibility of challenging
McCallum and North Side for the district championship.
With Hackberry gone, they had better forget about winning football games and concentrate on winning the sportsmanship award given annually to the student body that
displayed the most sportsmanship at athletic contests.

Jim and Joan ate lunch together at the Red Mill on
Wednesday. For the first time, Jim himself brought up the
subject of Hack Jones.

"Is your friend Hackberry cutting Miss Miller's English
class?" he asked as casually as he could. "He hasn't been
there the last two days."

"He's not even in school," Joan told him.

"What's the matter? He looked healthy as one of his billy goats Monday."

"Don't try to be funny," Joan snapped back. "He's not sick—not physically anyhow. But the poor boy is pretty low otherwise. This eligibility business has really hit him hard. It has knocked him out of any chance for an athletic scholarship. And if he can't go to college—which he can't without a scholarship—what does high school matter?"

"Everybody needs to finish high school," Jim pointed out. "Hack ought to realize that."

"Jim, he has to make his own living. And the only way he has to do it is to get back to rodeo competition. And that means buying a roping horse. And well-trained roping horses come high. Working full time at the riding stables, he at least has a chance to make and save some money."

Jim was silent a moment. Then, annoyed at having to show his ignorance, he asked her why all the stress on the horse. What was a roping horse, anyhow?

Joan sighed and gave him one of her "oh-you-stupid-thing" looks before she explained. "The mount is just as important as the roper," she told him. "The horse keeps the rope taut while the cowboy ties up the calf. The best cowboy in the world can't post a decent time in calf roping if the horse doesn't perform to perfection."

"Hack did all right in Cheyenne, you said. Didn't he have a horse then?"

"His brother's. And it was killed in the accident when his brother was killed. That's why Hack quit the big-time rodeo circuit—it takes a big stake to get started on your own, and he didn't have one."

"Does he have to *own* a horse?"

"All calf ropers either own their horses or make deals with people who do own them. Hackberry told me about Toots Mansfield, who was the world's champion for a while. He started out on the big-time circuit roping off a horse that belonged to Tony Salinas—and Salinas got half the winnings for the use of his horse. A deal like that makes getting rich on the rodeo circuit a pretty slow business."

"We'd better get back to class," Jim said abruptly. He was silent as they walked the half block back to school. Why had he never even thought of Hackberry's being hopeful about a college scholarship? He just hadn't, and suddenly he knew why. Why had he hurried to warn Coach Pearson? A sense of duty as co-captain of the team—nuts! He knew exactly why he had done it; why try to kid himself any longer? He had seen Hack only as a threat to his own football chances, never as a person with problems of his own.

Hack's appearance in the dressing room before practice that afternoon did not lighten the load on Jim's conscience. In fact, it grew heavier as he listened to Hack telling his former teammates how sorry he was that he had caused them to forfeit the Dexter game. He went on to thank them for their good times together. Especially did Jim writhe inside when Hack singled him out for special thanks —Jim had helped him more than anybody, the lanky redhead declared, and he surely did appreciate it.

As Jim led the way out to the field, Hack followed along still talking about his hopes, even his prayers, that the Rovers would win every game from now on and how he would be rooting for them to beat McCallum and North Side so that they could represent the district in the playoff.

"It'll take more than hopes and prayers, Hack," Jim said awkwardly. "It would take *you* to do that. We'll miss you, boy."

As he turned away toward the field, Jim was muttering viciously to himself. "And you, Jim Carter, you fine co-captain, saw to it personally that your team wouldn't have Hackberry Jones. You knocked Riverside out of the competition so you could be a big shot."

Not even to himself would he say what hurt even worse. The harm to Hackberry Jones personally was greater, more cruel, more unforgivable.

"What have I done? What have I done?" Jim kept asking himself all week. And he wished he did not know the answer.

9

HELP FROM A

LAWYER

❖❖❖

The Red Rovers were favored over Travis, even without Hackberry Jones. But Jim still felt more nervous than usual as he and Sandy Stone led the pre-game calisthenics. "If we lose this one, it's all my fault." Those words kept drumming in his head. He worked especially hard on his passing during the warm-up, but he was not pleased as they returned to the locker room. It was harder to throw to Dick Eudaly than to Hackberry, even in practice; Hackberry could catch them no matter where they were thrown.

Jim kicked off, then made the tackle himself as Travis halfback Skipper White almost broke free. White was the real scoring threat of the Travis Titans; he could outrun any other player on the field.

Sandy Stone called the defensive signals for the Rovers.

Jim and Jack Mitchell, the other linebacker, spread wide to help the ends contain White. Mr. Zanoba had felt confident that his line could stop the Titans in the middle, and so he placed the ends and linebackers in a box formation to stop the end runs.

Two dive plays netted the Titans only three yards. Jim saw the quarterback frowning as he looked over the Riverside defense, and he could understand why. As Jim moved to his position, he slapped Sandy on the rear. "They can't score without going wide," he told the center, "and we're not going to let them outside. Don't worry about that."

The next play fooled everyone on the field. Just before the ball was snapped, the Travis quarterback stepped aside. The snap went to the fullback, who kicked it low and hard. A quick kick from the 40-yard line! The pigskin bounced and rolled all the way down to the Riverside 9 before the referee whistled it dead.

Jim called a dive play, then a fullback follow, trying to work the ball out to a less dangerous position. But Travis was determined too. Jim would not pass from so deep in his own territory, obviously. So the Titans were safe in using a seven-man line, with the linebacker and halfbacks in close.

The first quarter dragged to an end—three pile-ups and a punt again and again. Riverside stayed in its own territory too much to risk Jim's passing. The Rover line held Travis, and Mr. Zanoba's box formation kept the Titans from breaking loose around the ends.

A bone-crushing tackle by big Sandy Stone in the middle of the second quarter finally gave Riverside the break they had been waiting for. Stone hit speedy Skipper White just at the instant a lateral did. The pigskin bounced free, toward Travis territory. End Mutt Allison fell on it at the Travis 42.

First and ten in Travis territory! And here came Bill Baxter running onto the field. Weary Jim Carter gratefully walked toward the bench. When the running plays wouldn't work, they needed Bill's surer passing.

Bill called his bread-and-butter play, the run or pass option, on first down. The seven-man Travis line rushed hard. The slight sophomore twisted and feinted, but the rushing end would not let him get outside. Eudaly was covered, by one man again. Bill had to cut back inside and struggle to hold his loss to only three yards.

The sideline pass was Bill's second down call. Again came a rush by the Travis line. Only a high, out-of-bounds throw stopped another loss.

Mike Geary ran the fullback draw on third down. The Titans were fooled, all right. Mike burst right past two linemen and into the secondary. But after only a five-yard gain he was horse-collared and slammed to the ground by the linebacker.

Coaches Snow and Pearson looked grim as Jim went back in to punt. And who could blame them? The Crimson offense had made only one first down all night.

Coach Pearson left Jim in the next time Riverside got the ball. Rich Conover made thirteen yards on a reverse. But immediately Travis tightened up again. Jim tried to pass. Neither Dick nor Ed Holloway, who was in for Gordon, was open. With seven linemen rushing him, Jim could not wait for anyone to break into the clear. Nor could he find running room. He finally had to "eat the ball" for a 7-yard loss.

On third down, Jim completed his first pass, but only to safety-valve Mike Geary. Big Mike rambled for twenty-two yards before being pulled down by three pursuing Titans.

That play, however, was the only ray of hope, and that hope died quickly. The half ended with Baxter at quarterback, but just as helpless as Jim had been.

As the disheartened Rovers trudged to the locker room at the half, Jim almost expected an explosion from the usually calm Mr. Pearson. After all, they had not come even close to scoring against a team that was supposed to be weak. Instead, Mr. Snow diagrammed the Travis defense. "It is basically a seven-diamond," he explained, "the oldest defense in football. But also one of the most effective, unless you can pass them out of it. Since both ends rush, the flats should be open, but you have to pass quickly."

Mr. Snow also changed two pass patterns to counter the Travis defense. He instructed Eudaly and Holloway to double-team the defensive halfbacks by running straight at them, then splitting off.

Chris Zanoba praised his stubborn defense, and then Jim and Sandy tried to pep up the Crimson team. Even though Jim acted enthusiastic, he felt no confidence as they returned to the field. He was not sure he was capable of executing the quick passes diagrammed by Mr. Snow. And Bill was not doing much better—he simply was not tall enough to pass effectively over seven onrushing linemen.

The second half began as a carbon copy of the first, for the teams exchanged punts without making a first down. Then Riverside finally began a drive. Rich Conover swept right end for twelve yards, then Mike Geary made five on a draw play. Jim faked the draw again and completed a pass to Dick Eudaly for eighteen yards. Mike Geary made five on a follow, then nine on the power sweep. Jim himself then carried on the pass or run option for a first on the Travis 4-yard line.

The Travis line was obviously tired. They were not rushing nearly so hard, and the Crimson offensive line was clearing out gaping holes. With first and four, Jim decided on the power sweep. He and Mike executed the play perfectly, and Geary bulled his way into the end zone.

The silence from the stands told Jim that something was wrong even before he saw the official's red flag. A clipping penalty! The referee stepped off fifteen long yards, back to the 19.

Jim called the sideline pass and had Eudaly open. But he threw short, and a Travis halfback cut in front of Dick and intercepted. Jim finally pushed the Titan out of bounds, on the Travis 38. Riverside had lost their best scoring opportunity.

Stopping that drive apparently inspired the Titans. They

held again, forcing Jim to punt as the quarter ended. Travis almost scored on the first play from scrimmage; White broke free for twenty-seven yards before Steve Goodman caught him. But the Crimson defense held again.

Travis stopped the next potential Riverside drive after two first downs. Jim had tried to pass with third and four and was thrown for a 7-yard loss. Neither Eudaly nor Holloway had been open, even running Mr. Snow's split-off pattern.

The Rovers got the ball back with five minutes left in the game. "This is it, men," Jim urged his teammates in the huddle. There was time left for only one sustained drive.

A power sweep and a sideline pass carried the ball to midfield and a first down. A trap play, with Conover carrying, made six yards; then Chet Gordon carried on a cross-buck for five more. Geary went for five, and then came the halfback dive for three. Jim was trying to exploit the tiring Travis line, hoping to break somebody loose.

He hit Eudaly on a look-in, then carried again on the pass-or-run option. He had wanted to pass, but Eudaly was covered. The Titans were finally double-teaming him, trying to force Riverside to stay on the ground so that the clock would keep running. Mike Geary's third down power sweep was stopped three yards short of the first down, and Jim called for the kicking tee.

The line of scrimmage was the 18, and Rich knelt to hold at the 24. Jim wished that his first field-goal effort of the year could be a little closer, but he was confident that the thirty-four yards was not beyond his range. If only he could kick it straight!

He never got the chance to find out how straight his kick was. A tall Travis end broke through and leaped high. His outstretched hand just barely touched the ball, but it was enough to deflect it well to the right of the crossbar. The ball bounced harmlessly out of the end zone, and the jubilant Travis team took over at the 20.

In less than two minutes, it was all over. The Travis quarterback simply fell on the ball, perfectly happy to tie favored Riverside.

The 0-0 tie counted as a half game won and a half game lost in the district standings. Powerful North Side was still undefeated. Riverside might as well consider itself eliminated, as soon as the district committee met and voted the forfeit of the Dexter game.

The Riverside dressing room was as quiet as Miss Miller's English class. Even the ebullient Mr. Snow had nothing to say. The coaches quietly checked bruises and minor injuries as Julius Koen gathered equipment for the trip home. On the way out, Mr. Pearson called Jim aside and talked softly to his despondent quarterback. "Don't take it too hard, Jim. You played a fine game. It's more my fault than yours. I built our entire offense around one boy, Hackberry, and now that he's gone . . ."

Jim looked away to hide the tears in his eyes. He appreciated Mr. Pearson's concern, of course. But there was not another comment the coach could possibly have made which would have hurt Jim Carter any more.

Jim did not mention the Saturday night dance to Joan, nor did she express any desire to go. Since it was her idea that they stop dating steadily, it shouldn't bother her, he figured. As for himself, going to a dance was the last thing he wanted to do. This had been the most miserable week of his life. Seeing his teammates and Joan and the other girls so long-faced over the disappearance of Hackberry Jones, watching football change from enthusiasm and fun to dogged, do-your-duty work—and, worst of all, knowing that he, Jim Carter, had triggered the whole business—he wished he could just quietly disappear.

He was grateful that his parents did not question his staying in on Saturday night. He went to his room, turned on the radio, and picked up a book. The radio went off quickly, though, when a "sports capsule" turned out to be speculation about the probable district winner, now that Riverside had lost Hackberry Jones; the book never was opened. His favorite records also failed to distract his thoughts.

His reasoning that someone else would have found out about Hackberry no longer seemed as logical and convincing as it had last Sunday and Monday. And reporting his suspicions to the coach out of a sense of duty—that was not his true motive, and he was tired of pretending it was. He had reported Hackberry's winnings in rodeos so that

Riverside would have to depend again on Jim Carter for offensive leadership and spark.

He knew now that he could not carry that load. Nor could Billy Baxter without Hackberry Jones as a receiver, and the concentration of the opposing secondary on covering the split end. No other Red Rover could draw two opponents out of a play. Jones couldn't block—golly, no— but he took out two opponents singlehanded. Who else could do that? Who else consistently blocked out even one man on every down?

Jim turned off his light early and tried to sleep. Even discounting the effect on Riverside's football hopes, his quick report to the coach had been a terrible thing. He certainly never intended to keep anybody from being able to go to college, to interfere with a person's ability to make a living. Tall, friendly, trusting Hackberry Jones sure didn't deserve a blow like that.

By the next morning Jim had decided he had to talk to someone, to try somehow to undo at least part of the damage he had done.

He followed his father outside, picked up a hoe, and pretended to be willing to help with the weekend yard work. The story came out haltingly at first. He was not ashamed of what he had done, he struggled to explain, but of *why* he had done it. His selfishness had spoiled his team's chances, and that was bad enough. But worse still was what he had done to Hackberry. What kind of a captain was he? Could he possibly accept and wear a letter jacket with a star on the sleeve after this?

Mr. Carter understood his feelings, but did not try to minimize his guilt. The big harm, he agreed, was to Hackberry personally. As a lawyer, Mr. Carter felt sure that there was some way he could help Hack. There was bound to be a way Jim could make partial amends, at least.

"Thanks, Dad," Jim said quietly. "I feel better already."

"You might feel even better if you confessed to Hackberry what you've done," Mr. Carter suggested.

"Maybe so," Jim agreed. "With you to help, maybe things won't turn out to be so bad after all."

"Now buck up, Son," Mr. Carter advised. "Don't let one mistake ruin your season. You've failed once as a team leader; don't let it happen again."

Jim didn't wait for his father to get into the house Monday afternoon. He started asking what had been done by the time Mr. Carter got out of the car.

"I wouldn't say I've actually accomplished anything yet," the lawyer said. "But I know that Interscholastic League rule about prizes backward and forward. And I have talked to both Mr. Steward and Coach Pearson. They expect the meeting Wednesday night to produce nothing but a quick vote against Hackberry, of course."

Jim's face fell. "That's what I expect, too. I was hoping . . ."

"Oh, I'm not through yet," Mr. Carter added. "I couldn't make a living as a lawyer if I gave up on my clients this quickly. Even if there is evidence against them, I have to stick with them and do what I can or I'm not worth any kind of fee. I haven't talked to Hackberry yet. Right after dinner we'll find him and see if we can use what he has to say."

Hackberry was not at the stables. But when Mr. Ed Hudson found out what the Carters wanted to see the boy about, he immediately offered his help.

"That boy's like my own son," the wrinkled old man observed. "Guess I know as much about his business as he does—maybe more. Come on in to my office here. I'll get my records for you."

The "office" proved to be an old-fashioned rolltop desk in the corner of the barn. From one of the drawers Mister Ed produced a dog-eared account book.

"Here it is," he said. "The records of all the rodeos we've had at Oak Hill—eight, in all. Hack's won first money five times."

Mr. Carter made an entry in the small notebook he always carried in his pocket.

"How much does that amount to, in money, that is?" he asked. "Much more than twenty-five dollars, I'm sure."

"More than twenty-five dollars?" Mister Ed gave a short laugh. "No, not yet. In fact, Hack may not ever collect that much for his trouble."

"Not ever? I don't understand."

"Simple," Mister Ed answered. "Hack and I are equal partners in the rodeos. The other calf ropers pay entrance fees, but Hack doesn't. When the others win, they collect all the entrance fees less ten percent. Hack doesn't collect anything. He's roping for the house—if you understand what that means."

Mr. Carter nodded. "I see. Do the other contestants know that when Hackberry posts the lowest times, their entrance fees go to pay expenses?"

"Sure," Mr. Hudson said. "Of course, if we ever make a profit on the rodeos, Hackberry would get half."

"Whether he wins the calf roping or not?" Mr. Carter asked quickly.

"Sure," Mister Ed told him. "But there haven't been any profits." He scratched his head. "There isn't much interest in rodeos around here. Fifty, maybe a hundred people come out and pay six bits to watch—we'll never make any money that way. But Hack and those other young fellows get a chance to practice some, and maybe someday they can make it in the big time. It's worth it to me."

Jim had watched his father's face carefully during all these questions and answers. Now he could sense the older man's excitement, though he had not heard anything himself that seemed to add up to a solution to the problem.

Mr. Carter stopped his note-writing and asked Mr. Hudson another question. "Then Hackberry has not collected any prize money since those two days at Cheyenne? When was that?"

"That's right," Mister Ed grunted. "That was summer before last."

"Has he entered and won in any other rodeo since then —during the last year, specifically?"

"Nope." Mister Ed shook his head. "Well, rightly, yes

and no. He entered at Houston. But he didn't win. He was roping off my horse and that old mare just isn't that good a horse. Hack just quit after that. He decided he wouldn't spend any more money on entrance fees and expenses until he had a horse that would give him a fair chance. Just here at Oak Hill—he won't enter anywhere else till he can afford a good roping horse."

Mr. Carter's smile broadened. "That's fine, that's fine," he said. "As I see it, Hack is eligible to play high-school football. I'll get permission to speak for him at the district committee meeting Wednesday, and I believe we can get this whole business cleared up. Meanwhile, Mr. Hudson, get that boy back in school."

"I sure will," Mister Ed promised.

Coach Pearson called Jim out of class the next morning. He had talked to Mr. Carter and was very pleased with the news. But, the coach said, he did not want the Rover squad to know that Hackberry might be declared eligible after all. To raise their hopes and then have them dashed again would make things even worse. Jim promised to stay quiet, and he kept his word.

Wednesday night Jim waited on pins and needles. His father returned home from the meeting shortly after nine o'clock.

"You have your split end back," he announced calmly. "Now from here on out, you play like a captain, not a jealous sophomore."

*　　*　　*

The news traveled rapidly. Jim was greeted at school the next morning with much backslapping, handshaking, and "Isn't it great about Hack?" from every side. The threesome of Joan, Beth, and Lucy nearly knocked him down when they rushed up, grabbed him, and tried to start some sort of impromptu "victory dance."

"We've got our boy back, Jim. Look out, McCallum and North Side," Lucy sang out.

"And your father did it! Oh, I love that man," Joan squealed. "Weren't we lucky to have a fan who is a good lawyer and also understands how important Hackberry is to the team?"

"Yes, sir," Jim agreed. "I sure feel better about everything this morning—Hack, and football, and the championship and—well, just everything."

And thank goodness, Jim thought, Joan and the others didn't know what that "everything" included. Already it was easy to push the memory of his own selfish thoughts and actions out of his mind, and he could not help enjoying the absence of the anger and resentment that had so often welled up in him at the mention of Hackberry's name. It felt wonderful to share the enthusiasm of his classmates.

The hubbub in the dressing room before practice that afternoon would have swept anybody into the spirit of excitement and optimism. Hackberry's appearance was greeted with cheers and shouts as the entire squad almost mobbed the rangy redhead.

"Hey, men!" Jim finally made himself heard. "Remember, he doesn't have much meat on those bones of his. Don't hurt our split end—we need him against McCallum, and without bruises!"

As they filed out toward the field, Hack fell in step with Jim and his face took on a serious look.

"Jim, there's something——" He hesitated as if not quite sure what he wanted to say. "Well, I want you to tell your dad for me—I'll tell him, too—but could you just tell him—I sure do appreciate what he did for me?"

"Sure, Hack," Jim replied. "I'll tell him. But he already knows that we *all* appreciate it. And we'll all team up to *show* him, and everybody else—on the football field."

"That's right," Hack agreed heartily.

After practice had ended and the dressing room was almost empty, Coach Pearson called Jim into his office.

"The boys looked good today, didn't they, Jim?" the coach asked pleasantly.

"Yes, sir, mighty good."

"Having Hackberry back has given the whole team a lift," the coach remarked. "Your father did a masterful job with the committee last night," he went on, his eyes twinkling. "In fact, he laid a beautiful trap and led them right into it."

As Mr. Pearson explained the details to Jim, his grin grew wider and wider. Mr. Carter had wangled from the committee a unanimous vote that the Interscholastic League rule must be enforced "to the letter"—a vote which seemed to doom Hack's chances at the outset. Then the attorney went on to stress that the crucial figure was $25. If Jones had won and collected more than that amount in the past twelve months, the committee had no choice but to vote the Riverside star ineligible. But if Jones had *not* received that much, then the same rule exactly should prevail. It did not matter what he *could* have received, but what he actually got. The committee could find no flaw in this argument. Then Mr. Carter had triumphantly produced copies of Ed Hudson's records. Hackberry's first place showings in Oak Hill competition had not netted him one cent.

After that, the committee decision that Hackberry was eligible was a mere formality.

"And we have you to thank for that decision, Jim," the coach concluded. "For without your father's help, I feel sure it would have gone the other way. Thanks to you and him, we're back in the running again."

"Thank you, sir," Jim said quietly. As he left the gym, though, he said to himself what he could not say to Coach Pearson, "Yes, but it was also thanks to me that the trouble came up in the first place—and thanks to me that we were ever out of the running."

That hurt. He could only hope that the hurt would go away as he redoubled his efforts to play like a captain, and that he was determined to do.

10

A TEAM AT LAST

◆—◆—◆

The roar of the crowd was so loud that Jim was stunned as he led the Rovers onto the field. McCallum and Riverside were traditional rivals, of course, but never had they drawn this big a crowd. Even the temporary bleachers in the south end zone were full. Riverside alumni from all over the state were gathered to celebrate homecoming and watch their team fight for the district championship for the first time in years.

The blue-clad Knights kicked off to Chet Gordon, who was stopped at the 22. Baxter, Jones, Holloway, and Wayne ran out to take over the Red offense. Jim was worried about Bill; the small sophomore still looked nervous. In the locker room before the game Bill had been scarcely able to talk. It was not hard to understand: a sophomore quarterbacking for the district championship!

McCallum had come to play, no doubt of that. They had championship hopes, too. The Knights had lost only one game, and if they could beat these upstarts from across the river, they would be in second place.

Mike Geary was stopped cold on the first play, then lost two yards on the power sweep. But on third down Bill Baxter showed his stuff. He rolled out to pass, dodged a rusher, then reversed his field, taking the Knights by surprise. Bill rambled sixteen yards before the McCallum safety man pushed him out of bounds.

The Knights had been well schooled on the dual threat of Bill Baxter and Hackberry Jones. Their outside linebacker covered Jones in the flat, while a halfback protected him in case the lanky wingman tried to go deep. The ends did not rush, but played Bill cautiously, forcing him to go inside. Only a fierce block by tight end Mark Chalmers had cleared Bill for his long run.

At the sideline pass Hackberry was open, even with two Knights trying to cover him. Jim noticed Dick Eudaly shout encouragement to Hackberry as the lanky end returned to the huddle. Jim himself was shouting "Way to fire!" at Bill Baxter. "Maybe we're finally thinking more about the team than ourselves," Jim said to himself. The tie with Travis while Hackberry was gone had made an impression on the seniors.

Pat Wayne made three yards, then Bill overshot his mark on an up-the-middle pass attempt. The Knight linebackers blitzed, throwing Bill for a loss, and Jim ran out to punt.

It was a high punt with no runback, and the Crimson defense took over. Jim and Jack Mitchell were at linebackers, Frank Thomas and Mark Chalmers at ends, Sandy

Stone and Rod Billings at tackles, and Joe Kotura at middle guard—this first-string defense hadn't yielded a touchdown all season.

They stopped the Knights at midfield, but only after two first downs. McCallum ran the I formation with a split end. Most of their plays featured the fullback leading the blocking for the tailback, powerful Joe Krause. They came right over Jim on one or two plays. He made the tackles, but each time he felt as if he had been run over by a Mack truck.

The Red Rovers took over again on their 18. For an awful instant it looked as if Bill's sideline pass had been intercepted; the Knight halfback actually had the ball in his hands, then dropped it. The near interception must have shaken Bill, too—he called two running plays and then Jim went out to punt again.

McCallum threatened early in the second quarter, pushing to the Riverside 26. A fumble ended the Knight drive. Joe Kotura recovered the loose ball after Mark Chalmers rushed from his end post and forced the Knight quarterback to rush his handoff.

Then Bill Baxter and Hackberry Jones mounted a drive of their own. Baxter threw to Jones for seven, to Holloway for eleven, then to Jones twice again. Bill had obviously regained his confidence; he was throwing the ball like a bullet. He ran himself on the pass or run option for fourteen yards to the McCallum 45, the first penetration of Knight territory.

A fluke stopped this Riverside drive—at least that is what

the boys on the Rover bench called it. Bill threw to Holloway across the middle. It was a good pass, but a little behind Ed. He turned and it hit his shoulder, bouncing high
in the air, right into the outstretched arms of a McCallum
defender.

Jim shook his head in disgust as he ran out to his defensive post. Gosh, what a sorry break! And against this
McCallum team, they needed every chance for success they
could get.

The Knights opened up with time running out in the
half. A pass gained eighteen yards, then seven on an end
sweep. Krause made eight on a flair pass, with Jim making
the tackle. "Watch those delays, Jim," cautioned Sandy
Stone. "If that big clown ever gets up a full head of
steam . . ."

Jim grunted his agreement; they had all seen the movies
of Krause's 80-yard run against North Side.

Second and two. The Knights tried a long pass, but it
was wide. The Red Rovers dug in to stop the first down.

The McCallum quarterback faded back to pass again.
Jim began checking off eligible receivers, then saw the
pass. It was short, to the tight end who had simply turned
around at the line of scrimmage. Jim timed his tackle perfectly, hitting the Knight end just as the ball did. He
looked anxiously toward the yardage chain to see if the
Knights had made their first down.

Then he heard the roar from the McCallum stands, and
saw Ed Krause streaking toward the goal line, with Steve
Goodman in vain pursuit. "Oh, no!" he groaned aloud.

The old flea-flicker play, and he had been fooled completely. The McCallum end had not even tried to catch the ball, but just flicked it off his fingertips to Krause, who had been following at full speed.

McCallum converted the extra point. 7-0.

The half ended without the Rovers scoring. They had begun to move again, but a holding penalty and two incompletions forced Jim to punt once more. The Knights easily held onto the ball until the half ended.

Jim did not know what kind of lecture to expect from the coaches at halftime. He felt as if the Rovers had played good football, but still——

Instead of a lecture, Coaches Snow and Zanoba were actually smiling as they stood in front of their team. "Boys," Coach Snow declared, "I never thought a team could lose a touchdown by being too aggressive on defense. Jim, you and Steve played that silly pass perfectly. You're supposed to hit a receiver when he catches the ball. Don't feel bad about that touchdown; it just goes to prove that football plays are designed to score even if the defense does everything right."

The coaches seemed unworried about McCallum's one-touchdown lead. Their calm assurance made it easy for the boys to build up their own spirit and confidence. By the time the official gave the two-minute warning, there was no doubt in Jim's mind that the Rovers were going to defeat McCallum.

However, the Knights had plenty of spirit of their own. They stopped Riverside's first drive, then moved to the Red

Rover 40 before being stopped. End Mutt Allison was the hero of the Rover defensive stand; he diagnosed a screen pass to Krause, and threw the big Knight tailback for an 8-yard loss. McCallum punted into the end zone, and Bill Baxter and his crew took over on the 20.

Bill threw to Hackberry for a first down, then across the middle to Ed Holloway for another. He was lengthening his aerial efforts; the Knights double-covered Hackberry with a linebacker and a halfback. Once Hackberry went out beyond eight or ten yards the linebacker dropped off, leaving only the halfback to cover him. And, Jim knew, there wasn't a high school halfback in the state who could cover Hackberry Jones all by himself.

A fumble stopped this Riverside drive. Bill threw to Mike Geary, his safety valve, and big Mike headed for the sidelines. Perhaps he started running before he really had the ball; he was hit about the line of scrimmage and the ball bobbled loose. A blue-clad Knight recovered on the McCallum 37.

Jim groaned as he ran out to his defensive position. It sure looked as if the football gods were against them tonight!

Krause ran into the middle for two, then for three. The Knights could afford to eat up the clock with running plays. There were less than three minutes left in the quarter. On third down the Blue quarterback faded back, then handed to Krause on the draw play. Joe Kotura, Sandy Stone, and Jim all seemed to meet the ball carrier head on.

The resulting 3-yard loss forced the Knights into another punting situation.

The punt was low, to the Riverside 25. Chet Gordon fielded it on the dead run and headed for the sidelines. Chet was a little ahead of his blocking wall or he would have gone all the way; the only Knight between him and the goal line shoved him out of bounds on the Riverside 46.

Another chance! Jim and the defensive team stood on the sidelines, joining the stands in shouting, "Go!"

Little Bill Baxter acted like the calmest person in the stadium. On first down he faded straight back, looking for a receiver. He dodged a rusher, then was brought down. But he didn't have the ball. He had handed off to Mike Geary on the draw play. His feint had been so perfect that even Jim hadn't seen it from the bench. Mike lumbered into McCallum territory, to the Knight 45.

Second and one. Bill liked to throw long with second and short yardage, and the Rovers on the bench knew it. They were tense with excitement before the ball was snapped. Hackberry ran the long pattern all right, and Bill faked a pass to him. But instead of following through Bill simply tossed the pigskin over the heads of the onrushing Knights, again to big Mike Geary. Mike was finally brought down on the McCallum 36.

First and ten. The stands were in an uproar now; Bill had to hold up his hands to quiet them before the Crimson team could hear the signals. He rolled to his right again. The Knights weren't rushing so hard now; they had been fooled two straight times, by the draw play and the screen pass. Nobody knew just what to expect from the slight Riverside quarterback.

It was the look-in pass. Hackberry fielded it perfectly, then fell to his knees. Bill had apparently instructed the lanky wingman not to risk a fumble. The play gained five yards, to the McCallum 31. With second and five, Jim expected Baxter to try a longer pass. Instead, Bill rolled to his right again, on the pass-or-run option. He had no intention of passing; he looked once downfield, then lowered his head and charged right past a startled defensive end. It was another first down, on the McCallum 25.

Bill rolled to his right again, but threw this time. His pass was perfect, to Hackberry on the right sidelines. This time the tall end did not fall to his knees. He feinted to his right, then reversed his field and cut back towards the middle of the field. He was hit by a desperate lunge at about the 20, but he didn't even slow down. A defensive halfback caught Jones at the 5, but couldn't bring him down; Hackberry just kept twisting and driving forward. Jim knew it was a touchdown even before the referee raised his arms.

Pandemonium reigned. Hackberry was almost crushed by the red-jerseyed boys trying to hug him. Jim grabbed Bill Baxter and almost knocked him down in his excitement. Only Bill seemed calm; the slightly built youth just barely managed a sheepish grin as he returned to the bench.

Jim started out for the extra-point try, then was called back by Mr. Pearson. "We go for two," the head coach said calmly. Jim gulped, then ran out with Conover. The fake kick they hadn't used all year!

Rich knelt with the kicking tee as the Knights grimly prepared to try to block Jim's kick. But Rich rose with the snap, rolling to his left. Jim hurried to protect the passer. Rich started to run, then changed his mind and threw. The pass was high, and Hackberry was covered by two men. It could not be complete, but it was. Hackberry leaped high in the air and caught the ball on his fingertips. He fell to the turf hugging the ball to his chest as two Knights tried vainly to knock it loose. 8-7, Riverside ahead!

The rest of the game was hazy to Jim. It seemed that Krause and the other Knights just kept coming at him. Time and again he lowered his head and charged into the ball carrier head-on. It was grim, hard-nosed football, but Jim and the Rovers held the Knights. Rich Conover went in at safety and broke up two long passes. Rich seemed to know just what play the Knights would run; on running plays he charged up and assisted the tackle at the line of scrimmage, but he never let a pass receiver get behind him.

Ten minutes, then six, then four. It seemed to Jim that the game would never end. McCallum punted, and Jim returned to the bench, hoping for a little rest. He was so tired he could hardly pick up his feet. Rich was just as tired, as was Chet Gordon; the three did not even talk as they sat together on the bench.

But one play later, Jim had to go back out. Bill Baxter had rolled to his right, hoping to run out the clock without risking a fumble by handing off. He made four yards before the converging blue jerseys swarmed him under. The whistle blew, but Bill did not get up. Mr. Pearson and Julius Koen ran out to the field.

"Get up, Bill," Jim shouted hoarsely from the sidelines. Chet and Rich, together with the rest of the Red bench, joined in his plea. But Mr. Pearson shook his head and motioned for two linemen to assist Bill off the field.

Spectators on both sides of the field rose and applauded as Bill was carried off the field. Bill wouldn't go down to the locker room; he shook his head violently and protested until his two helpers deposited him in Mr. Snow's canvas-backed chair.

Jim blinked and ducked his head to hide the tears in his eyes. Gosh, what a ball game that little scrapper had played! He deserved every bit of the applause that still filled the stadium.

"Come on, gang," Jim urged his teammates in the huddle. "We've got to win this one—for Bill."

Mike Geary went for five, then Chet Gordon for six on the reverse. The power sweep with Geary carrying added five more, then Jim on the quarterback sneak went for seven and another first down. The Knights couldn't stop this angry Crimson attack. The Rovers were blocking and running savagely, thinking only of punishing the team that had injured their sophomore quarterback.

In fact, Jim caught himself thinking about calling the halfback pass. They could score, he was sure of it. The Knights were in an eight-man line trying to stop the Rover ground attack and cause a fumble. But with only two minutes left—it would be stupid to pass.

"Calm down and make sure you hold onto the ball," Jim advised his teammates. He called two dive plays, then the power sweep. Mike Geary powered his way for eleven yards and another first down.

Another quarterback sneak. Jim simply fell on the ball. He wasn't going to risk a fumble, not with less than a minute left in the game. "The sneak again," he ordered, "with a long count." Jim could hear the stands counting off the seconds remaining as he waited for the snap from Red Billings. "Eleven, ten, nine, eight——"

At the snap Jim fell on the ball again. He hugged it to his chest even as he heard the gun sound to end the game. He was going to present the game ball to Bill Baxter personally, and nobody was going to take it away from him.

11

ANOTHER CHANGE AT QUARTERBACK

◆―◆―◆

The crowd of football players gathered around their usual table in the school lunchroom was glum. They had received shocking news from Mr. Pearson that morning—Bill Baxter's ankle was broken. The sophomore quarterback was out for the rest of the season.

The broken bone was a surprise. True, Bill had left the McCallum game with a leg injury, but he had been sure it was only a slight sprain. In fact, Bill himself had assured the team that he would be ready for practice Monday. He had sprained his ankle before, he told them, and soaking it in hot Epsom salt solution would fix it right up. But Dr.

Bradford had been concerned about the swelling, and had insisted that Bill report to the hospital for an X ray. There was no doubt that a small bone in Bill's ankle was fractured.

Monday's practice was in shorts and tennis shoes. Mr. Pearson quickly put a stop to all talk about the North Side game. After all, he pointed out, they had to beat Central first. If Central knocked them off, North Side wouldn't matter.

Jim spent the week running plays from the spread formation. He took a football home with him each night, too, and spent at least an hour practicing passing in his back yard. He was improving; now he could throw one out of two through the swinging tire hanging from a big oak tree in his back yard. But still, he thought to himself, nobody would mistake him for Bill Baxter. Somehow he just couldn't catch on to the quick delivery. He had to take his time and aim before he could throw straight.

The week passed quickly. With practice every afternoon and passing at night, Jim did not really have time to worry about the upcoming game. He had to spend two hours a night studying, too; Mrs. Carter was an ex-schoolteacher who believed that classroom work was more important than football, even when the team had a chance at the district championship.

Friday finally came, the day of the game. Jim and Hackberry were both reprimanded in Miss Miller's English class for not paying attention; it was easy to think of pass patterns instead of sentence structure on a game day.

Mr. Pearson warned the team about overconfidence and looking ahead to North Side, then sent them out to open the game.

"Why is he worried about overconfidence?" Jim asked Chet Gordon as they waited for the school songs. "I'm not overconfident—I'm not even confident!"

In spite of Jim's misgivings, Central wasn't a tough opponent. The Bobcats had lost three district contests by lopsided scores; North Side had beaten them 42-0.

The Red Rover ground game clicked from the start. Conover returned the kickoff to the 30, then made seven yards on a cross-buck. Mike Geary gained twelve on a power pitch, with Jim leading the blocking. Jim carried himself on the quarterback option for five, then handed off to Gordon on a dive play for six more. Mr. Pearson had instructed Jim to run out of the Straight T until he ran into difficulty, and the Rovers were simply overpowering the smaller Central team.

They moved to the Bobcat 30, and then Jim decided to pass with third and five. He called the pass-or-run option and rolled to his right. Dick Eudaly was wide open, but so was the right side of the field. Jim turned the corner, then lowered his head and plunged straight ahead for ten yards and the first down. That was not spectacular running, like Bill Baxter's, Jim thought to himself with satisfaction, but it sure got the job done.

The passing threat opened up the Central defense; Mike Geary powered his way to the 12, carrying two Bobcats with him. The halfback sweep gained a first down on the 8, and Central called time out.

"Gentlemen," Hackberry Jones announced formally as they gathered around the water bucket, "we are doing real well." Jim grinned, amused at Hackberry's language and manner. "And we are doing well," he said to himself. Why shouldn't they be? This was the kind of football they had planned on playing, until the unexpected appearance of Hackberry Jones made them into a championship contender. And, in all honesty, without Hackberry and Bill— well, Riverside would have had a losing team, though certainly Jim Carter would never have said so before the season. Now they were running over Central, and could win the championship by beating North Side, if a certain Jim Carter could play quarterback.

Rich Conover joined in Hackberry's levity. "Mr. Jones," he proclaimed in a pompous manner, "my associates and I appreciate your profound appraisal of the situation. However, we are disturbed at your shocking misuse of the King's English. Miss Miller will undoubtedly be equally disturbed when she is informed of your shortcoming Monday. *Very* well, *extremely* well, *quite* well—but please, Mr. Jones, not *real* well."

The mock distress on Hackberry's face brought chuckles from the team.

"Come on, you clowns, let's get back to work," instructed Jim. "We can have a seminar on English after the game." Jim was pleased, despite the gruffness in his voice. The rest of the team had accepted Hackberry as a first-class teammate, just as Jim finally had. They had a *team* now, not a bunch of seniors fighting juniors and sophomores for first-string positions. He was also pleased at the laughter; Mr. Pearson had said many times that a relaxed team did not make mistakes. There was no doubt that this Crimson team was relaxed, even with first and goal to go, and the big game of the season awaiting them next week.

Mike Geary scored on the power sweep on the next play, with Jim and Sandy Stone leading the blocking. Jim converted, and the Red led 7-0 after only four minutes of play.

Riverside scored again in the second quarter, again on running plays from the Straight T. It was harder to move against Central; the Bobcats had drawn into an eight-man line, simply daring Jim to pass. But Mr. Pearson instructed his senior quarterback to play a cautious game. North Side was not playing tonight, and their whole coaching staff was surely in the press box, hoping to find a way to stop the Riverside offense. There was no need to open up and expose their spread formation plays, not when Central didn't pose much of a threat.

Jim scored the second touchdown himself, on the quarterback bootleg from the 14. It was one of Bill Baxter's pet plays—while the halfback and the wingman went to the right, the quarterback faked a handoff and kept the ball behind his hip while running to the left. The success of the play depended on the quarterback's fake. If he could trot unconcernedly to his left, looking at the halfback, he could convince the defense that he had handed off and draw them to the other side of the field. Jim and

Rich Conover worked the fake handoff beautifully, and Jim was wide open. He scored without a hand being laid on him.

Mr. Pearson replaced Jim with sophomore Don Wilson on defense in the second quarter. Don had good size and speed, and needed the experience. There was another consideration also, as Coach Pearson explained to Jim. "You're the only quarterback I've got now. We can't take a chance on your getting hurt, at least not while you're playing linebacker."

The second quarter closed without a further scoring threat by either team, and Riverside had a 14-0 lead at halftime.

A fumble recovery by Mutt Allison on the Bobcat 38 set up another Rover score in the third quarter. Jim threw his first pass of the game, hitting Eudaly on the sideline pattern. Dick broke free and went into the end zone, but the referee ruled that he had stepped out of bounds at the 29.

With second down and one, Jim was tempted to throw another pass, but Mr. Pearson left Hackberry sitting on the bench, obviously wanting Jim to stay on the ground. The inside reverse, with Conover carrying, made four yards and the first down. Mike Geary made seven on the fullback follow, then six on the power sweep. Hackberry entered the huddle, with instructions that Jim could pass if he wanted to.

Jim started to call the sideline pass, then changed his mind. If his passing had improved, it would be smart not to let the North Side coaches know it. Riverside would have a better chance if the North Side team thought that Jim could not pass at all.

He called the halfback pass instead. Rich rolled to his left, looking for Hackberry on the sidelines. Hackberry was covered, but Chet Gordon was wide open across the middle. Chet caught the pass in the end zone, without a white-shirted Bobcat within ten yards of him. Three Central defenders had covered Hackberry, forgetting that the Riverside patterns always called for at least two receivers.

Jim's kick was good again. Riverside 21, Central 0. The second- and third-string sophomores and juniors played the rest of the game for the Rovers, although Jim stayed at quarterback. They almost scored, too—Larry Johnson, a sophomore halfback, broke free to the Central 10-yard line, but lost the ball on a fumble on the next play. Central finally scored against the second-stringers with four minutes left in the game. It didn't matter to the Crimson team or their coaches—the 21-6 victory was satisfactory. They were already thinking ahead to next week and the championship game. Even if the team had not had such thoughts, the chant from the stands would have reminded them: "BEAT NORTH SIDE!"

Mr. Pearson began practice Monday with films of North Side's last two games. They had an offense much like the Rovers', except that their split end, Bob Carruth, was used even more than Hackberry. He was the leading scorer in the district, and had set a new state record by catching six touchdown passes. Jim watched the movie of the North

Side-McCallum game with fascination—Carruth caught passes with two men hanging all over him. It looked as if the tall, swift end just could not be stopped.

Mr. Snow then read a newspaper clipping to the team, from Sunday's *American*: "North Side," the sportswriter flatly declared, "will be this year's district champion. All that stands between the powerful Northmen and an undefeated season is the Riverside Red Rovers, also undefeated, but once tied. The Rovers, having lost their star sophomore quarterback, Bill Baxter, can't stay on the same field with the Vikings . . ."

"Fellows," Mr. Snow remarked, "we have two choices. We can believe this self-proclaimed 'expert,' and give up and play dead, or we can go out and play football. Do you believe him?"

"*No!*" shouted the team as they ran out to the practice field.

Practice lasted until dark for three straight days. Mr. Pearson drilled both offense and defense without pads, stressing sure execution of plays. He assured the Rovers that they could win, but only if they could stop Carruth. The Viking passer was a crack marksman, almost of professional quality. Don Burton threw to other receivers, of course, but his principal target was Carruth. Carruth and Burton had grown up as next-door neighbors, Mr. Pearson explained, and Burton knew Carruth's "moves." If the opponents tried to gang Carruth by covering him closely with two or three men, Burton would pass to his wingback or tight end, who ran a pattern much like that of the River-side offense.

Mr. Pearson's whistle closed the Tuesday practice earlier than Jim expected. The coaches called the team together for a blackboard drill to outline the strategy for the North Side game.

"Men, listen carefully. We have come up with a plan that we think will fix Mr. Carruth. We are going to gamble that Hackberry Jones can stop Carruth singlehanded if we put him on defense. If Jones can stop Carruth, and you fellows will rush Burton, then we'll stop their passing attack. And I don't think they'll be able to run against us."

Jim was stunned. Hackberry on defense! He recognized the strategy, of course. Hackberry would be a "free safety," much like that used in the professional leagues. His task would be to guard Carruth, with no zone or other respon-sibility to worry about. Jim listened intently as Mr. Pear-son continued:

"Of course, since Hackberry will be playing on defense, he won't be available as much for offense. He can't last both ways if he has to follow Carruth on every play. That means that you, Jim, Rich, Mike, and Chet, have to score from the Straight T. Hack can come in for a pass or two, but not much. The Straight T will carry the bulk of the offense. And, gentlemen, I can promise this—no matter what happens to Carruth, we can't win if we don't score!"

Jim almost never went to sleep Tuesday night, worrying about the North Side game. Mr. Pearson had placed the team's chances for a district championship squarely on his shoulders. He had to make the Riverside offense work. He could count on the Riverside running game to make yardage, but could they score? He remembered how much trouble they had scoring in the earlier games and couldn't help wondering.

Jim practiced his passing furiously that Wednesday afternoon, throwing to Eudaly and Chalmers from the Regular T and to Hackberry and Holloway from the spread. He still wasn't satisfied, and he could tell the coaches weren't. He had no difficulty with the short look-ins, but was not very successful with the sidelines and longer passes. If they were going to concentrate on their running game, it was the longer passes that mattered—they would only be passing on long-yardage plays, or when they caught the Vikings up close and wanted to catch them by surprise with a "bomb."

After practice Jim reluctantly walked up to Hackberry and asked for his help. Hackberry agreed eagerly; the lanky junior wanted Jim to do well even more than Jim did.

Jim threw three sideline passes, then attempted a cut-and-go, where Hackberry broke for the sidelines, stopped, and then cut back toward the middle and long. Hackberry motioned for Jim to sit down and explained that he had discovered Jim's problem.

"You throw it straight enough," Hackberry told him, "but you throw to the wrong place. You throw *to* me, not ahead of me. You can't throw right at the reciver—he's too well-guarded for that. You've got to throw ahead of me, whichever way I'm cutting, and you've got to guess about that some of the time.

"It's like roping goats," the lanky end continued. "Throw at the critter and he'll dodge your rope every time. He knows to cut sharp when he hears the rope swishing. He goes one of two ways, either right or left. You gotta guess which way the four-legged fool is going, and throw there, have the loop waiting for him. Let the goat run into it. Calf roping is different, because a calf turns and then goes straight. You can rope a calf from a horse, since you know how to lead it. But a goat—nobody could rope a goat from a horse. They've got a way of their own. Even a good roper like my brother missed a lot. Nobody could catch a goat with the first loop."

Jim caught on fast once he understood Hackberry's method. Hackberry went out like a goat. He did not run a pattern, but just hoped to get open. He ran out, broke into the clear, and then looked for the ball. Of course he didn't know which way he was going to cut; that depended on what the defensive man did.

Jim quickly caught on to the sideline passes, realizing why he had missed before. Hackberry didn't cut until the last second. You had to throw at the sidelines, at least five feet away from Hackberry. He could turn and cut to the sidelines, beating the ball every time.

After several hours of practice against the Riverside defensive team Wednesday and Thursday, Jim and Hackberry began completing most of their flair and look-in patterns, and even some long out-and-down efforts. The trick,

Jim decided, was to watch the defensive men instead of Hackberry. If he could watch them and decide where Hackberry would be open, he could just throw to the open spot. Hackberry seemed to sense where he would be open and cut instantly. Usually he was waiting for the ball, wide open, in spite of the two defensive men assigned to guard him.

After Thursday's passing drill both coaches looked pleased. The team sensed the coaches' confidence, and spirit built up. Jim was nervous, of course. Who wouldn't be when he was the quarterback in a championship game the next day? But still he popped Mark Chalmers with a towel as the junior walked out of the showers. Jim was feeling much more relaxed and confident than he had ever expected to be on the eve of a big game. If only he and Hack could catch North Side by surprise with a couple of passes!

12

THE

CHAMPIONSHIP

GAME

◆—◆—◆

North Side fielded the opening kickoff. They lined up in the spread with Carruth, tall, slim, and graceful, split to the left. Hackberry slouched only three steps away, watching Carruth's every move. The orange-jerseyed visitors tried to exploit Carruth on the first play. He went left, then straight out and long on the cut-and-go, with Hackberry right beside him. Burton saw Carruth covered and tried to run, but Joe Kotura and Mutt Allison upended him for a three-yard loss. Burton shook his head in surprise as he slowly got to his feet. Obviously he hadn't expected

Riverside's stringbean defensive man to be able to guard Carruth man-for-man.

There was another pass on second down. Both Jim and Jack Mitchell were rushing from their linebacker posts, and Burton was almost trapped. He cocked his arm and got off a hurried toss. But Hackberry was on target, covering the ace North Side end. He slapped the pass down. Incomplete.

The Vikings ran on third down, unwilling to risk a pass in their own territory while they were uncertain about this strange Riverside defense. How could one man guard Carruth, when two had been unable to stop him all year? The end sweep gained only two yards. North Side had to punt.

Rich Conover fielded the ball at midfield and was tackled instantly. The Viking defense was big and strong; they stopped Mike Geary for no gain, then held Chet Gordon to two yards. Jim started to call the power sweep, but changed his mind when he saw the Viking ends and halfbacks box the corners. North Side was apparently well schooled on Jim's bread-and-butter play.

He called the halfback pass instead. It was a perfect choice. The North Side halfbacks stayed close, expecting Rich to run. Mark Chalmers cut across the middle and was wide open, three steps behind the Viking safety. He did manage to get a hand on the ball, but Rich's pass was a little high and wide. The Riverside fans groaned as the ball bounced to the ground.

Mark was almost crying as he returned to the huddle.

"Gosh," he groaned, "we had them. If only I could have hung onto the ball!"

"It wasn't your fault," argued Rich. "You were wide open and I threw it badly—and I had all the time in the world, too."

"Both of you shake it off," Jim advised. "We didn't score, but we scared the heck out of them. They're liable to be a little shaky for a while."

Jim's punt was high and long, and Carruth was forced to make a fair catch on his 15. "That's good kicking," Chet congratulated Jim. "Thirty-five yards from the line of scrimmage and no run-back."

North Side tried another long pass to Carruth. Burton seemed certain that Carruth would break free with only one man guarding him. Again Hackberry was right on top of the Viking end. Burton had to run, and again was thrown for a loss.

Jim and Steve Goodman hugged Hackberry as he returned to his defensive post. "Hackberry," said Jim, "you ought to be playing for the Green Bay Packers."

Hackberry ducked his head to hide his obvious pleasure. "Naw," he drawled, "it isn't much. He's just like that calf I was telling you about—cuts and runs in a straight line."

North Side made a first down on a quick pass to tight end Fritz Kornig, then tried a look-in to Carruth. This one was complete, but for only a 4-yard gain. Carruth was covered on the next play, a sideline pattern, and Burton's hurried toss to his safety valve went incomplete. On third down Jim brought Burton down for an 8-yard loss, as the Viking quarterback was again unable to find an open receiver. Burton just couldn't seem to realize that Carruth wouldn't be open any time North Side needed a sizable gain.

There was no score as the first quarter ended. The Rovers had stayed in good field position, even though their Straight T wasn't gaining much against the Vikings. Jim was really punting—he kicked from the Riverside 42 down to the North Side 9 as the quarter ended. North Side ran three running plays, then punted back to their own 43.

Mike Geary made three yards, then was stopped for no gain on a power sweep. Jim completed a sideline pass to Eudaly, but the pass was short and Dick had to catch it coming back. He was tackled two yards short of the first down. Jim chose to punt rather than give up the Rovers' field position, and North Side took over on their 17.

The Crimson defense held again, but not until North Side had gained two first downs. The Vikings had almost given up on Carruth. Instead, fullback Joe Spaulding hit the line again and again. Quarterback Burton was a good runner himself—he went wide on an option play for eight yards. But when Burton again tried to pass to Carruth, Hackberry was there. Jones's defense and Mark Chalmers' fine play on an end sweep forced the Vikings to punt again.

Another exchange of punts used up five more minutes of the second quarter. The Rovers took over on their 41 with seven minutes left. Jim anxiously looked toward the bench for instructions. They weren't moving the ball with their running game against this tough Viking defense, and he wanted to score before the half. Coaches Snow and Pearson were in consultation on the sidelines and did not send in instructions. Jim called a pass on his own.

He faded back and to his right, looking for Eudaly on the sidelines. Dick was covered, but Mark Chalmers was open across the middle, waving his arms. Jim's pass was true, and Riverside had a first down on the North Side 40.

Riverside fans roared as Hackberry Jones came out to the huddle with his unmistakable gait. North Side promptly called time out to adjust their defense, and Jim sank to his knee. Golly, he was tired! Playing both ways was hard work, especially when he had to rush Burton every play from his linebacker post.

Jim could sense the excitement in the huddle. This Rover bunch had confidence in Hackberry and him. They had seen the passes work in the practice sessions, and felt sure Jim could connect in a game. Jim felt his nervousness building up; these guys wouldn't let him down. They would block for him on both passes and runs. If only he didn't let them down!

Play resumed, with the Vikings in a five-man line, and a linebacker and halfback covering Hackberry Jones. Jim passed on first down, but didn't even look at Hackberry. Instead he threw a jump pass to tight end Mark Chalmers across the middle. Two Vikings hit Mark quickly, but the play still gained five yards.

The cut-and-go was planned for Jones, but Hackberry was covered. Jim ducked a rusher and sprinted to his right, faking a pass. He could not scamper like Bill Baxter, but he could move when he had his speed up. He cut inside and scrambled for six yards, with Mike Geary contributing a crushing block on the Viking linebacker.

First and ten on the North Side 28. Jim rolled to his right again, looking for Hackberry. The split end was covered, and Jim was hit by a rusher. He stumbled free, then lobbed the ball to safety valve Mike Geary. Big Mike lumbered on for seven yards.

Jim called the second down play in the huddle. "Power sweep left on three." He was hoping to catch the Vikings expecting another pass, but he guessed wrong. A tackle bounced off Jim's shoulder block and downed Mike for a two-yard loss.

Third down and five! The fans were on their feet now; Jim was conscious of the roar as he stepped behind the center. But he couldn't distinguish the "Go!" coming from the Riverside fans from the "Hold 'em!" of the North Side section. The sideline pass went to Jones. Jim threw it perfectly, but he had guessed wrong on the cut. The ball went out of bounds on Hackberry's right after the tall split end had turned and cut to his left. Jim shook his head in dismay. He had expected to guess wrong sometimes, but this was sure a bad time to miss.

Fourth down. Jim called time out, hoping for instructions from the bench. But no substitutes came out, only Julius Koen with the water bucket. Mr. Pearson believed in letting his quarterback call most of the crucial plays. He said that the team would understand if a quarterback called the wrong play, but no team could win if it lost faith in the coach. Besides, they were going to school to learn how to think as well as win football games.

Jim looked at the scoreboard clock, then made up his mind. With only three minutes left in the half, it was unlikely that North Side could score. It would be better to take a small lead into the locker room than to have the half end scoreless.

Rich Conover ran quickly toward the bench for the kicking tee. The ball was almost squarely between the hashmarks, and there was no wind. Jim was almost relaxed and confident as he waited for the snap.

The kick was perfect. Riverside led 3-0.

North Side roared back, outraged at trailing this upstart Riverside team. Burton ran for six, then Spaulding for five. With better field position, Burton decided to go to the air. Carruth cut across the middle, with Hackberry on his heels.

The pass was perfect, right at Carruth's chest. But the long arm of Hackberry Jones snaked in front of the Viking end, deflecting the ball. It hit Carruth in the shoulder, bouncing high into the air, and into the cradling arms of Rich Conover on the North Side 35.

Two minutes were left in the half. Jim hurried the team out of the huddle, into the spread formation. He faded back, but was rushed hard by both North Side ends. Jim faked the pass, then lowered his head and charged straight into the middle for five yards before the defensive secondary picked him up.

Second down and five on the North Side 30. Jim called

the same pass pattern, the out-and-down. Hackberry was almost open at the goal line, but Jim saw an opening at the right side and ran again, this time for seven yards, to the 23.

"Go, Big Red!" roared the stands. The Vikings pulled into a four-man line with five defensive backs, expecting a pass. Jim faded back again, but handed off to Mike Geary on the draw play. Mike bulled his way to the 18. Jim called time out to stop the clock.

When nothing came from the bench, Jim decided on the halfback pass. Three Viking halfbacks were covering Hackberry, so Rich ran out of bounds for a one-yard loss to stop the clock with thirty-seven seconds left.

"They got me outnumbered," Hackberry apologized in the huddle. "I can't get open against three men this close to the goal line."

Jim studied the Viking defense. If a pass wouldn't work, they had to run, even with the time almost up. "The power sweep right," he instructed. "Hack, you cut across to the left, wave your arms, and make noise. Try to draw their whole team over there with you."

Jim's improvised play almost worked to perfection. Hack cut to the left, waving his arms frantically for the ball. Jim pitched back to Mike Geary, who raised his arm as if to pass to Hackberry before turning the corner. Jim didn't see the rest of the play; he threw a block on the Viking linebacker, who fell right on top of him. Mike broke loose, but was caught from behind at the 9 and brought down on the 6. He had scarcely hit the ground before he was on his feet, waving for another time out.

Mike barely caught the referee's attention in time. There were six seconds showing when the clock stopped.

Jim studied the angle as he waited for play to resume. The ball was resting on the west hashmark, as far to the right of the crossbar as it could possibly be. That was surely a bad angle for a short field-goal effort.

The snap, the kick! Jim thought he had missed; it was low and to the left, but still between the uprights. The referee's hands went up and Jim could have hugged the man in the striped shirt.

Riverside led 6-0 at the half.

Mr. Pearson's halftime speech was terse and to the point. "You fellows are playing great football. All you have to do is stay after them. But I warn you, it'll be rougher next half. They know we're after them, and that we can stop Carruth. Now they'll play with everything they have."

The Vikings came out with fire in their eyes. Their coach must have instructed them that Carruth wouldn't be open; instead of running pass patterns, the star receiver was blocking on most plays from his split-end post. The Vikings drove to the Riverside 35 before being forced to punt after a clipping penalty.

North Side's defense was fired up too. The Rovers made only five yards on three running plays, and Jim had to punt. He was not about to do much passing from his own territory, not with Riverside in the lead.

The Vikings stormed back. Spaulding made five on a

crisscross, then the halfback went wide for four more. Burton picked up the first down with a quarterback sneak. A jump pass gained seven. Jim felt helpless to stop the fierce Viking attack. He could see the plays coming, but he was being blocked by two men.

Burton took the snap, then handed off to Spaulding. No, it was a fake—Burton still had the ball and was going wide, and Mark Chalmers was cleanly blocked out. Jim shook off a block and started pursuing Burton.

Steve Goodman was blocked out; Burton was going all the way unless Jim could catch him. About three yards behind the swift Viking, Jim started to leave his feet in a desperation dive. At that instant a lanky red-shirted youth came out of nowhere and hit Burton with a crushing tackle.

Jim blinked in amazement. "Good Lord, is that you, Hackberry?" He helped the stringbean end to his feet. Hackberry grinned sheepishly, rubbing his jaw. "Well, somebody had to stop him—I guess I got excited," he explained, almost defensively.

Jim had to grin. Only Hackberry Jones would apologize for making a tackle!

But North Side scored later, despite Hackberry's brilliant pursuit. Hack had made two more tackles. He was proving himself an effective defensive end, even against running plays. His amazing balance made it almost impossible for the Vikings to block him out, especially the way he fought off blocks with those long arms. But Riverside couldn't stop the Viking attack. North Side scored on a screen pass to Spaulding for fourteen yards, and a quick pass over the middle to tight end Kornig. The Vikings had driven seventy-five yards without their star split end's ever touching the ball.

The Viking kick was good. North Side led 7-6.

Hackberry explained his sudden adeptness at defense during the time out at the end of the third quarter. "You know, I always thought you had to be mad at somebody before you could hit them. I never got mad playing football, and never wanted to hurt anybody. I got mad at a goat once, and hurt the critter roping him too hard, and I never wanted to take a chance on hurting anything else. But then I got scared Burton was going to score, and tackled him hard—it didn't hurt him or me. It's like bulldogging a steer; you can bring 'em down without trying to hurt them. Tackling people is more fun than catching passes—it's like bulldogging, only it's harder and there's not much chance of getting yourself really hurt."

Jim didn't really understand, but he pretended to. How could anybody think that you had to be mad before you could make a hard, clean tackle or block? That was the whole idea of the game!

The Vikings held Riverside again, when Jim lost three yards trying to pass and Dick Eudaly dropped a sideline pass. The Rover defense held this time, but North Side punted to the Riverside 18.

Jim shook his head in the huddle. They were running out of time, with only ten minutes left and eighty-two yards to pay dirt. He was going to have to get something going, and quick!

The first downs on running plays improved Riverside's field position, but used up over two precious minutes. Jim completed a sideline pass to Eudaly, but a holding penalty wiped out the play and moved the Rovers back to the 25, with a first and twenty-five.

In came Hackberry Jones. The Vikings shifted to a four-man line to stop the expected passing threat. Jim sent Hackberry deep along the left sidelines, then handed off to Mike Geary on the draw play. Mike followed Sandy Stone's crisp block and gained twenty-two yards against the surprised Vikings.

The delayed cross-buck gained seven and the first down in North Side territory. Jim was willing to exploit the Vikings' four-man line for all that it was worth. There was plenty of time to score on running plays if North Side would stay back and wait for a pass. There had to be a hole somewhere if the Vikings were using two or three men to cover Hackberry.

Rich Conover was stopped for no gain. North Side had shifted back to their usual six-man line, and Jim decided to pass immediately. The sideline went to Hackberry—he guessed right, hitting Hack just as he turned. It was the look-in this time; Hackberry was covered, but Jim threw to his left, and the lanky end made a diving catch for a six-yard gain.

First and ten. Jim guessed again in the huddle. The Vikings were concentrating on Hackberry, and he wanted to surprise them. He took the snap and rose up as if to throw to Hackberry on the look-in, then turned and rolled to the left. He had to cut inside; he could not outrun the opposition to the sidelines as Bill Baxter had. But he caught the linebackers moving over to help with Hackberry, and broke free into the Viking secondary. The North Side safety brought Jim down on the 24, after an 11-yard gain.

North Side called time out. Jim sank to his knees with fatigue. He could hear the chant from the Riverside stands now—"Carter, Carter, Carter!" He blinked with surprise. Gosh, now *he* was the hero. The fans just couldn't realize that Hackberry Jones was responsible for this Crimson offensive surge. With two Vikings following Hackberry out on every play, it was easy to gain. Besides that, Jones was making fine downfield blocks on every down. Of course, football fans never notice the downfield blockers. They think the ball carrier gets there all by himself.

The spectators had already forgotten Hackberry's fine play. In came Eudaly, and the long-legged Hack got only scattered applause as he left the field.

First and ten. A Viking linebacker broke through and stopped Mike Geary for no gain on the cross-buck. The halfback sweep gained only a yard as Rich stumbled, trying to turn the corner. Hackberry rejoined the huddle.

Jim faded back, looking for Hackberry on the sidelines. The split end was covered; he had been hit at the line of scrimmage and couldn't run his pattern. Jim dodged a rusher, then threw hurriedly to Mark Chalmers across the middle. The pass was short and bounced incomplete.

Fourth down. Jim and Rich took their field-goal positions without a huddle. Jim licked his lips nervously and wiped the sweat from his hands. If he never kicked again, he had to kick this one. The clock was still running; this would be Riverside's last chance to win the championship.

The kick was up—it was perfect! Jim gulped with relief. It felt as if somebody had just taken a 100-pound weight off his back. Then he was swarmed under by his red-shirted teammates and practically carried up the field to the kickoff position. Even Coach Pearson, usually calm under any circumstances, was pounding Mr. Snow on the back and shouting hoarsely.

The stands were roaring Jim's name now. "Carter, Carter!" Jim didn't even hear them. He concentrated on placing the ball perfectly on the kicking tee. He wanted this kickoff to carry into the end zone, and away from Carruth.

It was Jim's night, all right. The kick carried at least five yards deep in the end zone, and Burton kneeled with the ball. North Side had possession, first and ten from their own 20—if the Rovers could only hold!

A screen pass gained five. Back went Burton to pass. Jim and Mark Chalmers rushed hard, but Burton dodged and planted his feet for the long bomb. Carruth was there, about forty yards from the line of scrimmage, but so was Hackberry Jones. The two leaped high in the air, but Hackberry was taller; he reached the ball with an outstretched hand and deflected it away from Carruth, toward the sidelines.

Again Rich was there! He waited, then held the ball lovingly in his arms as he stepped out of bounds to avoid being tackled and risking a fumble. For the second time in the game, Rich had caught a deflected pass.

It was Riverside's ball on the North Side 40, with two and one half minutes left. Jim took his time, breathing deeply to calm himself down. He called a long count, then took the snap and fell on the ball. The Rovers stood in the huddle watching the seconds tick off the scoreboard clock. There was a 5-yard penalty for delay of the game. Jim carried again, just ducking into the tangle and falling on the ball. He wasn't going to fumble, not with the championship two minutes away.

North Side stopped the clock with a time out, then another as Jim fell on the ball a third time. Jim took advantage of the delay to wipe his hands and shoes with a towel provided by Julius Koen. He wanted to end this night for the Crimson offense with a booming punt.

The punt was high and long. Safetyman Don Burton couldn't run, not with the red jerseys pouring down on him. He signaled a fair catch and fielded the ball at his 15.

Burton had to pass now. Jim stationed himself and the other linebackers seven yards behind the line of scrimmage. "Let them gain some," he chortled to himself. "All we need to do is to stop the touchdown."

Burton threw to Carruth on first down. Rather, he threw towards Carruth—Hackberry had the split end tightly covered and Burton threw short to avoid an interception. His next effort was a long desperation heave to tight end Kornig, with only twenty-five seconds left. It was short, landing right in the hands of Conover. Rich fell on the ball, beaming with exultation at his third interception of the game.

The change of possession stopped the clock, but the game was over for all practical purposes. Jim and his teammates stood in the huddle and listened to the Red Rover fight song, then walked slowly up to the line of scrimmage. They didn't even take their positions, but stood there watching the clock tick off the seconds. Jim thought the scoreboard with the 0:00 shining from it was probably the most beautiful thing he had ever seen. Then he couldn't even see the scoreboard, as fans, players, and students gathered him up and carried him toward the locker room.

Joan caught Jim just as he reached the entrance to the locker room. Tears were still streaming down her face, which was flushed with excitement. Jim had to grin at her —only a cheerleader would be crying when her team had won the district championship. But Joan always cried when they won; girls were certainly funny when they got emotional.

"Oh, Jim, you were wonderful!" Jim had to push her away from him so she wouldn't ruin her red cheerleader's sweater on his wet, dirty uniform.

"Now, calm down, Joan. How about Hackberry? He won the ball game for us, and this wasn't the first one."

Joan was almost angry at Jim's defense of Hackberry. "Hackberry did fine," she admitted. "But you were the star. You won the game, with those wonderful passes and kicks."

The students surrounding them echoed Joan's statements. Jim didn't argue with them—he didn't want to be accused of false modesty. Surely, he thought, anybody who knew anything about football realized who made the difference. If Hackberry hadn't been there, covering Carruth like a blanket, and carrying two men out of every play— why, without him Riverside wouldn't have had any business on the same field with North Side.

It took Principal Robbins to move the crowd of students aside so that the elated Crimson team could finally get to their locker room. Jim grinned as Mr. Robbins climbed atop a handy soft-drink cooler and started making a speech praising the Rovers. The principal sure liked to talk—all it took was a crowd and he would make a speech, no matter what the occasion. The team took advantage of the diversion to slip into the locker room through a line of well-wishers and back-slappers.

The locker room was almost as noisy, even with only the team there. Photographers and reporters hounded Jim and the others as they stood congratulating each other. Nobody even tried to change his sweaty uniform; there was too much excitement to worry about dressing.

Jim moved over and sat beside Hackberry Jones in a corner. Hackberry was shy, and always managed to remain inconspicuous when reporters were around. He was apparently worried that he might say something that would sound silly in the newspapers, although he would talk as much as anyone with only the team around.

"Great game, Hack!" Jim said warmly, putting his arm around the lanky end's shoulders. "That was the best game you've ever played."

"Yep," Hackberry agreed instantly. "I did manage to give Mr. Carruth some trouble. And I caught a couple of passes—you threw them right to me. That practicing we did paid off, didn't it?"

"Sure did," Jim said softly. The two just sat quietly, enjoying the excitement and horseplay in the locker room, both filled with thought. It had been quite a season.

A tap on the shoulder woke Jim up from his daydream. Mr. Pearson was standing there, smiling. "Son, get dressed," the coach said. "There's a gentleman in my office waiting to talk to you. Coach Darrell Royal of the University of Texas."

Darrell Royal! The University of Texas! Jim was speechless with excitement. He had wanted to play for the Orange and White ever since he was old enough to know what football was about. Funny, though, during the last couple of weeks he had forgotten about the college scouts. The excitement of the championship race had pushed his own ambitions out of his mind.

"Don't keep Coach Royal waiting," said Mr. Pearson. "I've already told him you were a midterm graduate, and that he could talk to you as soon as the season was over. He must be pretty anxious to see you, to be here so quickly. You can talk in my office—that is, if you ever get dressed."

Jim nodded, already pulling off his jersey. He could get dressed all right. He might even be able to tell Mr. Royal something. He grinned at his own thought as he walked toward the shower. What would the Texas coach say about having his ends study goats!